JUSTICE

THE MCCOYS:
BEFORE THE FEUD
BOOK 4

THOMAS A. MCCOY

INTRODUCTION

After the successful raids on the Northern Army's stockpiles of Southern valuables, the McCoys waited until interest in finding who had executed the raids waned. At that point a group of the McCoys decided to go home to Kentucky. But at the end of their journey, they learned that Pinkerton detectives were hired to discover who'd taken the gold. They'd been lucky. Wiley sent a warning back to the ranch to the McCoys who were still there.

Tommy, one of the leaders back at the ranch put together a plan to deflect suspicion off of them once and for all. But most of the McCoys there thought the plan was too risky. They thought it safest to put a lot of distance between them and the ranch as quickly as they could with their bounty before the Pinkertons made it back to them. Those who left the ranch would not know if Tommy's plan to divert suspicion off their group would work.

More than half of the McCoys living on the ranch or on the surrounding lands near the ranch decided to hightail it to parts unknown after the warning came from Wiley that the Pinkertons would be there soon.

Three groups left the ranch, each one heading in a different direction. The bounty was only a small portion of what they were able to recover for the South. These included stockpiles of valuables that the Northerners had stolen from the South during the raids that were meant to help finance the war for the North.

Tommy's plan seemed to have worked for the time being. It appeared the McCoys had averted the suspicion from their family. The result of his plan had the Pinkertons headed in several different directions, following the trail of gold coins that were spent in various locations that were far away from the ranch and nowhere near the destinations the three groups were headed. Each group was on its own. The men were determined to hide their tracks. One group was headed to California, the other to Montana and the third was on its way to the Dakotas. These destinations were chosen because that's where gold was being discovered.

PROLOGUE

General Thomas Ewing Jr. had been building up his ranch just outside of Lawrence, Kansas for a while, having no idea that the Pinkertons were zeroing in on him with some questions about the stolen gold coins. He was busy inventing his future. He had aspirations of going into politics. He was savvy about money and good at impressing the right people. He wanted everyone to think he was a very, very important man. He had commanded a great many men during the war, and though triumphant, he was arrogant. He used his power to manipulate people to get what he wanted. Others knew this about him, but the general himself did not see himself in this way. He knew you had to be smart and sometimes clever to get what you wanted, but he would never think of himself as immoral or, for that matter, arrogant. He just thought that he'd been an impressive general during the war, and that he didn't have to shy away from his accomplishments.

His hope was to be a congressional representative for Kansas. He believed it would come naturally to him because of his efforts lobbying for the entry of Kansas into the Union as a Free- State. He had resigned his commission as general but remained on until the Army could find a suitable replacement. This explained why he was still in command along the Kansas-Missouri border when the gold was stolen from the military holding areas that were his responsibility. The gold was supposed to have been transported to Independence, Missouri for shipment east to the military headquarters. Ewing had never intended to tell anyone that the gold had arrived in Independence. Now he worried about how he could keep the recovered gold for himself that the Pinkertons had sent to him. How could he keep his name out of it? He knew he could blame communications and say he never knew that the gold was being sent. Then he could say the shipments never arrived anyway. After all, lots of shipped goods that he had been told were on their way, very often never arrived at the way stations for transport to Independence. Why should the gold be any different? But when it got recovered by the Pinkertons and then turned over to a sheriff and consequently sent back to him by way of his two trusted men, complications he hadn't planned on arose. He hadn't figured out yet how to deny receiving it.

He'd been thinking about how he was going to protect the gold and keep it for himself and decided he'd need to build an impenetrable storage area for it. He had sheets of steel shipped from Pittsburgh and riveting components for securing the walls together. He had even engaged Yale, the company that had invented the combination locking system in 1862, to install the new style combination locking system on the custom-made door that would mark the entrance of the vault. He built an extension onto his house and dug out the ground for the vault. Then he built a room over it when it was finished and he made the room his office and decorated it with fine furniture and books, including a Bible on a carved wooden stand. He'd made a trap door in the grand office that led to a staircase and the entrance of the underground vault.

When his military replacement arrived and he was finally relieved of his command, he retained his two trusted men from the stockpile sites. They already knew about the recovered gold and were trying to keep it hidden from the Army. He used these men to load the gold into the vault. This way there were only two people other than himself who knew what was inside. As a matter of fact, other than him, they were the only two people who even knew of the vault. They were also the only people who went to pick up the recovered gold from the local sheriffs who had received the recovered gold from the Pinkertons.

He explained away the underground work to his wife by making up some phony foundation repairs. He also hired ranch hands and a few gun hands. He used the cowboys for the work on the ranch which now had over 20,000 head of cattle and 5000 horses. The ranch also contained chickens and pigs that they used to feed everyone, plus they farmed many vegetables, which they canned and stored for winter, and used to feed the animals. The ranch was almost self-sufficient, but the general still had more work to do to cultivate more land to accommodate the number of animals and people that had to be fed in order to create and complete his dream ranch.

The gun hands, six in all, were assigned as his personal protection detail and as guards around the ranch house. He told them he'd made many enemies during the war and felt he needed protection. None of them knew of the gold that they were actually guarding.

He received the wire about the Pinkertons coming from one of the two trusted men whom he had always sent to check the telegraph offices. He was very concerned when he read the wire. Usually, he received wires telling him that the Pinkertons had recovered stolen gold coins and that they needed to be retrieved. Why, he wondered, were the Pinkertons bringing it directly to his ranch?

Something felt amiss. Rarely prone to worry, the general tried to imagine what they wanted by coming to the ranch. He didn't think it was a good thing.

Usually, the general didn't suffer any pangs of guilt about what he had done and about how he would use the gold to carry out his plans. But sometimes, late at night when his wife was asleep and all was quiet on the ranch, he wondered what it would be like to have less ambition. He was a man who had been raised a Christian, and he believed in the power of confession, of changing your life. Sometimes, he wondered if he had to come clean, whether he could tell the truth, give it all up for that chance to redeem some of his choices. On nights like this, he could often be found reading the

Bible by candlelight.

But usually, he never thought about his choices—whether they were good or bad. He just thought about how to safeguard his treasure and how to execute his plan to be elected a representative of Kansas and beginning—really beginning—his political career. He'd already been a strong military officer, a Free-State advocate and the first chief justice of the Supreme Court in the state of Kansas. He could practically taste it, achieving his next goal. All he ever wanted was to make a name for himself. And make everyone around him fear and respect him for his power.

Daily, he stood in his fine office, knowing the gold was below—right there, literally under his feet—and he looked out the big window onto his ranch, enjoying the endless sun in the endless sky, and he felt like he would soon get everything he ever wanted.

CHAPTER 1

DEPARTURES

The McCoys who decided to leave the area dropped off their portions of the gold to Tommy. Then they packed up. They were going to leave the next day. Few preparations were planned for the long journey. They all felt the need to leave quickly, with just a vaguely formed thought about where they wanted to end up. It was important that they took care to leave no trail by making sure not to use any of the gold coins. They needed to steer clear of the Pinkertons, lay low for a while and figure out how they could one day use those coins to build their dreams.

In all, three groups left the ranchland where they had once planned to create their new lives. The first to leave the ranch area were the California-bound men. They lost the most time in getting away. This group contained the three Williams and the two Georges. The three men named William nicknamed themselves Willy, Bill and Billy, and the two men named George went with "GH" and "G." This way there'd be less confusion while talking among themselves. It was not uncommon for McCoy families to have several members with the same names adding only Jr., Sr., or "Little," or "Big," either before their first name or as a suffix to avoid confusion during conversations. But if a couple of families got together for supper or a celebration, and there were children included who had similar names, the conversations could become very confusing.

Since there were not very many routes to choose from to get to California, and the weather was turning cold fast, the California group couldn't take on the mountain passes that were available during spring and summer. They decided they would go across Kansas to the newly formed town of Abilene and then down a route they had only heard stories about called the Texas Trail, or the Chisholm Trader Trail. Only one cattle drive had made an attempt hoping to arrive at the railroad in the City of Kansas, Missouri but the outcome was dismal.

By taking the southerly route, they hoped there would be fewer areas of mountainous terrain to cross. They also banked on the weather being warmer if they went down through the Texas, New Mexico, and Arizona territories to California.

"We can get supplies in Abilene," Willy said. Willy was tall and lean but strong. He was rarely seen without his hat, a black bowler that made his face look trustworthy and friendly. Out of the five who were traveling to California, Willy was the one who listened the best, and made the final decisions, especially when they argued. He was considered one of the smartest of the four other men he was traveling with, and took on the role of leading them along, but was always willing to change course if the others had arguments against his ideas, "If we head to Abilene and load up on supplies there," he said, "then folks in Lawrence won't spot us and tell the Pinkertons they saw us loading up our wagons and leaving the area."

The other men agreed it was a good idea to leave right away and load up their supplies in Abilene. They never had to discuss the obvious, that when they started out, they should stay away from Lawrence and anyone who might know them. They headed west towards Abilene with plans on going southwest to Wichita. From there, their idea was to head directly to Santa Fe. They didn't know anything about the routes or where they were going. All they knew was they had to get out of the Kansas area without being stopped by anyone wanting to check their wagons. Heading down to Wichita was a risky decision because the country was still a pretty wild place full of rustlers and outlaws, not to mention the Indians, the biggest cause of fear for people traveling west.

Willy reminded his group, so they'd always be on alert, that no matter what direction they went (except east where they couldn't go), that they would be confronting these kinds of elements. "Some places there won't be any Indians but remember that any which way we can go won't be a safe direction to travel."

The other men understood the warning and nodded silently.

Willy realized they were a pretty small wagon train with only one man per wagon. Anyone watching might have thought they'd be easy pickens. Then again, Willy figured that those looking to rob someone didn't know who they were or what they would be up against. What Willy didn't know was that soon enough their wagons would have to be traded in for pack mules and their wagon horses for oxen. He couldn't have known that they would have to join a much larger wagon train if they planned on making it to California. Plans had been hastily made and the men would all realize that soon enough.

On the fifth day of travel, feeling relieved that they had made it far enough away, they came upon a group of riders. Both groups stopped as they met on the trail.

GH asked the men on horseback, "You'ns come'n from Wichita?"

"Yeah, we been there," said one of the riders. "You got a long ways to go. Best be careful on this trail and especially when you get close to Wich'ta, cuz sometimes there's a lot of riffraff stay'n just outside of town."

"Okay," said GH. "Appreciate the advice."

The rider continued, "Abilene's tween here an thar an really just a stage stop, not a town but dangerous all the same. More ta worry bout in Wichita iffen you make it that far. And mind that you don't go anywhere by yourselves when you get there. That's why we're headed back to Kansas City, not worth gett'n killed to just punch cattle."

GH and his men looked at each other, listening now

as the rider continued. The more he said, the more Willy began to grow concerned.

"If yur think'n to go on further than Abilene, best not to, because of them Indians. They're worse than any outlaws."

"What about after Wichita?" Willy asked.

Another rider spoke up, "Wichita is just a two-bit cattle drive stopover, and just as disappointing as Abilene if not more so. And them injun's are thick once you get past there."

"Much obliged for the warning and we'll do just that," Willy said. "Y'all be careful where yur a headed."

The men, looking grim, nodded and continued on their way toward Kansas City. Willy and GH exchanged glances. Willy was starting to have some doubts.

The group going through Independence included Robesson, (now Roby which he pronounced like RowBee), Roby's brother, William C, (now just William), and Tom. They'd all fought together in the war. After their first stop, their goal was to head for Montana. They'd heard of gold strikes there, and it was a lot closer than California.

The City of Kansas group included Festus, Jones (now nicknamed Jonesy), James Sr. (now only James) and James Jr. (now just Junior). James and Junior had been the cooks during the time of the raids on the military stockpiles. They were going to the Dakotas first, then maybe over to Ohio.

• • •

The Pinkertons, meanwhile, sent word as far out as 250 miles, to as many of the larger towns to the north, south and east of Independence, Missouri wherever the telegraph could reach. Their message was always the same: Alert them to anyone spending gold coins. Through the telegraph, messages were returned reporting the places where gold was being spent. The Pinkertons, trying to be thorough, even sent word down to the Texas Rangers to keep an eye out for $50 gold pieces being spent. Any information, they said, will be checked out and followed up on.

CHAPTER 2

NEW LANDS

Having just heard about the Indians and other nefarious activities along their planned route, Willy was starting to wonder if they'd made the right choice in leaving the ranch and trying to get to California. To him it looked like the same thoughts were passing through the minds of the others as well. The old saying "in for a penny, in for a dollar" just didn't hold as much water when talking about your life being in the balance. Willy knew they were all thinking maybe it would be better if they turned back around, but no one said it. They wouldn't. Not yet at any rate.

Traveling across Kansas was like passing through a sea of short buffalo grass and barren land. Willy could feel the cold, especially when they camped at night, and though no one complained, he could tell everyone was tired and cold. By day as they rode on, the land rolled up and down, the vastness disappearing between the waves of the land, only to reappear when coming to the crest of the next wave. Rarely would there be any trees, though every once in a while, they'd see a lone tree standing tall as if in defiance of the desolate land. It was a good thing they all had two full water barrels in each of their wagons. The terrain seemed to be an endless expanse of arid desert but without cactus.

The landscape created optical illusions. Outcroppings that were small seemed large and looming in the near distance, only to reveal that they were many miles off and actually were of no significant size when the men came up to them. The nights, though, were something to be remembered—so many stars, such a beautiful black twinkling sky and the moon, when it was out, like a beacon. Those nights made the men feel exuberant about their journey and gave them courage. But then the day would roll out again, just like the day before, and the day before that, and they would once again question their choices.

Several times they saw small bands of Indians off in the distance sitting on their horses on top of a rise in the landscape, observing them. Once in a while the men would talk among themselves, wondering if the Indians were forming a plan to attack them. This fear kept them on high alert, watching their surroundings, looking hard at any movement in the distance, no matter how small they appeared. They came across a small sign saying, "40 miles to Mudd Creek" with the words "Mudd Creek" crossed out and under it written "Abilene." The going was slow in the wagons, but they were making good time anyway; on average 16 to 22 miles a day, depending how the horses were feeling. They were smart enough to bring grain and water for them, but that was starting to dwindle, and Willy was just then wondering if they had enough to get them to Abilene when they saw the sign.

"Well, that's good," said Willy.

The others expressed relief and they continued forward, knowing it would only be a couple of days before they could resupply the much-needed nourishment for the animals and give them some rest. The following day they began to see dust clouds in the distance.

"Maybe a dust storm coming on us," Willy said.

Silently, the men watched the clouds of dust and dirt in the air. Eventually, they realized the clouds were only rising up and then disappearing into the sky, not moving towards them. Though they didn't know it then, they were witnessing the second group of cattle to ever be driven up the Chisolm Trader trail. They finally figured out that the dust was cattle kicking up the dry land. It seemed as if the cattle were only a few miles away when in reality, they were almost 30 miles away heading to Abilene.

Toward the end of the day, they could make out the outline of what looked like buildings in the dusty air off in the distance. They decided to stop for the night, thinking they would make the rest of the distance the next day. During the night they could see a few small glowing orange fires dotting the land beyond the town that they knew was itself off in the distance. These, they knew, were the campfires of cowpunchers that had stopped for the night. They were all anxious to get to

Abilene and learn more about the Chisholm Traders Trail. They needed to find out just how secure for travel this new trail was for both their wagons and for their own safety.

Stories of the railroad coming through Kansas and Abilene were hopeful diversions for the people in the area. At the moment Abilene was still just a small group of buildings that served as a stage way station where the stage could stop and change horses and give the travelers some food and rest. Only recently had cattle been driven through the area on the way to the City of Kansas railhead for shipment to the east. It was disturbing for most travelers when they saw the sight of Abilene for the first time, thinking they were coming to a real town, only to find themselves looking at a few shanties and two buildings put together with the wood that had been hauled from Kansas City. There was a big corral and something that resembled a barn. For those who were savvy, they would know to be on the alert and keep a wary eye on the things they held dear to them. The California group had not considered this as a possibility. Willy expected to find a nice room to rest, and plenty of stores for the horses.

The next day, after seeing the cattle dust clouds, the men made it to the stage stop named Abilene. There were two stage lines running through the place. One of them looked closed for the day, if not forever. It was then they realized the big mistake they'd made in not stocking up on supplies before leaving Lawrence. The owner appeared when they came to a stop out in front of what looked like the main building. From the looks of the place the stage stop didn't have any supplies for sale and could only offer water. The stop owner told them if they needed meat, they could probably get a few head of cattle from the trail boss passing through or go hunting and get a buffalo or Antelope along their way. He offered them some feed for their horses and all the water they wanted for 2 dollars, saying they could get a hot meal of buffalo stew for a dollar if they wanted to come in and eat.

"We do have a small store called the Frontier Store," he said "but they only have a small stock of goods. We got a hotel, if you want to call it that and want to pay to stay there. I've got free bunks for customers, just a rack to sleep on, nothing fancy. Then again, there's nothing fancy at the hotel neither, where you have to pay."

Willy felt the regret as if it was a physical thing. It looked like the men did too.

The owner went on, "We got a place to wet your whistle. We call it Old Man Jones's Saloon. It's back off the main buildings, kind of hidden behind the rest."

Willy asked, "How often does the stage come through?"

"Not very often since the weather's started to turn cold," The man replied, "We got two lines run through here, but people don't go to Denver City in the winter if they can help it, the rides just too cold."

"We're not look'n to go that a way. Thought we'd go to Texas."

The owner quickly replied, "Might get as far as Wichita, go'n from here. After that ain't good odds on livin', but I don't think them wagons'll get over the

Texas Trail and make it to Wichita. Some are start'n ta call it "The Chisholm Traders Trail" cuz ole Jesse Chisholm used it to travel to Dover, Oklahoma, trade'n fur and such. That route was dang hard for the chuck wagons that came with the first herd of cattle to get here and probably ain't any real wagon road see'n most chuck wagons just follow along as near as they can to the herd. Doubt they followed the same tracks as those that came 'fore them on the tradin' route, but maybe there's some tracks you could follow by now." The man paused as if to catch his breath then said, "There's been one cattle drive come through, two now, count'n the one passin' today. Best try and talk to a trail boss to get the real low down on that."

He wasn't a man to give much help if it took him out of his way or if it involved work. He said, "Iffen youse get hungry I'll be inside. You can see where the feed and water for the horses is, help yourself to that." Finished talking he went back inside.

Billy looked at the others with what he knew was an expression of despair on his face. "Well, I guess all we can do is try and catch that trail boss and then hope he'll tell us the truth about the trail we need to take." He dismounted and started walking to open the corral gate for their wagons.

Willy responded, "No need to fret over it. There ain't no reason the trail boss should lie to us. Let's get these animals fed an' watered and then do the same for us. Tomorrow we can ride out and see if we can get some first-hand information from the men who've actually been on the trail. Maybe get us an idea of what we're go'n to be up against."

The corral was large, probably a full acre holding at least two teams of horses for the stage and some 20-plus mules. They pulled in and turned the wagons so that they would face the gate when they were ready to leave. Then they unhitched the horses, rubbed them down and went to the main building.

Once inside Willy asked the owner "What are all them mules do'n here?"

The man looked him square in the eye and with a seriousness Willy could see in his face, and he said, "Those are from a small wagon train that came through here over the summer and were attacked by Indians. The two people who survived, thanks to an army patrol passing by at the time, they was real lucky. Made it back here and told me where it happened."

"So what'dya do?"

"The two survivors took the next stage back to where they came from. I went out and rounded up the mules I could find. The patrol didn't have time to be chase'n em down. A few of them found their own way back here. Mules are smart that way. I figger I can sell'em to someone. Why? You interested?"

"Not sure yet," Willy said, "Just curious why you had so many, but I'll let you know. You said you had some grub we could eat, any left?"

The man smiled, and Willy knew that smile. The man was thinking about the money coming his way and the possibility of more, if he could sell them mules.

"Sure. Have a seat and I'll get it dished up fer ya."

After they'd eaten—a hot stew of indecipherable meats, supposedly buffalo and some kind of potato—the owner told them they could bunk in the second building down from where they were. The first building was for the stage passengers, but both were for sleeping and had eight bunks in each. The men, tired and disappointed, headed toward the bunkhouse.

Inside the building was a wood stove and firewood. Willy was glad for the warmth since it was getting very cold out there. There were indeed eight beds with dusty blankets and pillows. G took one blanket and shook it. There was such a cloud of dust that came from it, he started coughing and said, "I'm go'n to get my bed roll. It has to be cleaner than this."

GH added, "Probably why the sign we saw with the name crossed out for this place was "Mudd Creek at one time." Not exactly a name that shouts a reputation for how clean the place is." He was grinning as he finished. The others went out and retrieved their bedrolls. Bill put some wood in the stove to get some more heat going before he went for his bedroll. The chill was off the place when they got back, and they climbed into their racks and went to sleep.

Chapter 3

Choices

The next morning, they made their coffee in the bunkhouse. Too tired at first to say anything much, all five of the McCoys drank their coffee in silence. Each man seemed lost in his own thoughts. Willy felt bad because it had been his idea to come to Abilene and gear up. Now he'd put all of them in a bad situation.

"What's say we head out together and see if we can get any information round here," he said.

"And some breakfast," said GH.

The men nodded and got their horses. Mounting up they saw a dust cloud a ways out and headed straight for it. Getting close, they put bandannas over their faces to keep from breathing the dust. Coming up on a cowhand, the man put his hand on his gun.

Willy shouted out, "Whoa pardner, no need to be hasty, we're not bringing trouble, we just want some information about the trail you came in on."

He still kept his hand on his gun and answered, "What'd ya wanna know?"

Coming closer, Willy said in a lower voice, "We're planning on takin' the Texas or Chisholm Trail, whichever it is, down into Texas and wondered if it was good for wagon travel and if it was clearly marked."

The man took his hand away from his gun and looked at Willy for a long minute. Then as if deciding Willy and his men meant no harm he said, "I seen some of the trail the chuck wagon follows and it's not an easy route, but mostly I'm away from that out here with the cattle an' I didn't see anything that looked like a wagon trail. You'd be better off asking the trail boss or the cook. Our trail boss, we call him Mr. B, should be over by the chuck wagon. He always eats last. Head that away, bout a mile or so," he said waving his hand in the general direction.

"Okay, we'll do just that. Much obliged," replied Willy.

He turned his horse in the direction indicated by the cowhand, and the group took off. After a mile they saw the chuck wagon and rode directly toward it. Coming to the wagon, a man came around from the side of it saying, "Iffen you fellers are look'n fer work we got all the hands we need right now."

Willy said as they dismounted, "We jus' want some information 'bout the trail you'ns came here on. Is it good for regular wagon travel? And how do we find it and stay on it, if it is?"

The cook looked them over, trying to decide if they were rustlers wanting to know where to go find the next bunch of beef coming over the trail or if they really wanted to travel on it.

Clearly, he decided, they didn't look like rustlers and said, "I've been coming across it since they been takin it to get here. Only been two trips so far. It's get'n more worn in, but there's still lots a places you might lose it. There's a lot of rough places and it's slow go'n. Be pretty hard for a regular wagon, less'n you'ns have some oxen or had six horses a pullin it."

Just then a rider came up and got off his horse with an air of authority, and said, "Hey there fellers, saw you'ns ride up. I'm the trail boss of this here outfit, name's Mr. Irons. What can I do fer ya?"

The cook quickly said, "They's jus want'n to know if the Chisholm Trail is something they can travel over with regular wagons, Mr. Irons?"

Billy wondered why, if the range hands called him Mr. B, the cook called him Mr. Irons.

Then he noticed Mr. Irons looking hard at all of them.

"Well," he said. "ole Jesse used to make it with pack mules twice a year, haul'n goods ta Dover. You can't be a tin horn and stay on that trail, even on horseback. There's Indians and rustlers all along the way. We give them Indians some beef to let us come through, but we still never know how they'll be. This time they decided that they wanted more'n we offered and took almost half the herd and kilt ten of my men in do'n it."

Willy shuffled uncomfortably and glanced quickly at the others. He noticed them, eyes to the ground, hands in pockets, with worry on their faces.

Mr. Irons seemed like he saw that too. He went on, "You'ns don't look like tin horns, but you ain't cowhands neither. Iffen you have a choice, wait'll spring and then get you some pack mules or ox's and join a bigger wagon train head'n out the Santa Fe Trail and make that trip. At least that route has been traveled with regular wagons."

"You don't think the Chisolm trail is good?" Willy asked.

"Well, now," said Irons, "the Chisholm trail is not easy to follow and only a couple of cattle drives have come over it, this'n being the second and neither one did well. It's still not what you'd call a road. You'll find it over yonder. Can't miss it there. The chuck wagons have made a good two track to follow through here, but that don't last long. You can still see where someone's traveled though even after that, iffen you got a good eye, but it's rough. I wouldn't go that route iffen I was you, not with this little group. Them Indians will get ya first couple a miles in their territory. They'll be happy ta kill ya just to see if you had anything they might want and if you didn't, you'd still be dead, and they'd just leave ever'thing where you'ns died."

Willy felt the men tense behind him.

Mr. Iron's paused, then said, "I best be get'n back to the herd, good luck to ya!"

He turned and went to his horse and tipped his hat as he left.

Billy looked at the cook and asked, "Why do the range hands call him "Mr. B" if he calls himself Mr. Irons?"

The cook smiled and said with a chuckle, "The newer hands call him that for "Boss man," it's just shorter. The older one's know him as Branden, but can't say it without smiling at him, cause you know, full name's Branden Irons, an fer a trail boss, it's kinda funny to the hands, havin' yur boss named Branden Irons. Fer me, it couldn't be a fitter name for someone who drives cattle for a livin'."

Willy laughed. The others smiled a little and Willy could see they were being polite because he could tell they wanted to laugh.

Willy said, "Thanks for your help with the information 'bout the trail."

He turned to get on his horse, and they all mounted up. As the group rode away, once out of ear shot, Billy couldn't help but bust out laughing saying, "Can you imagine be'n named Branden Irons and punch'n cattle for a live'n."

The whole group—they'd been holding it in--burst out laughing. Thinking about that kept smiles on their faces all the way back to the stage stop.

The information wasn't what they had hoped for and all of them were worried about the big mistake they'd made not getting stocked up on supplies somewhere, not to mention the fear of Indians the trail boss had put in them. Later, after eating another bowl of stew from the owner of the stop, the men retired to the bunkhouse. As they sat around the warm stove, the California-bound men were about to turn in when Willy brought up the subject that was on all their minds.

"I don't know 'bout the rest of you, but I'm worried bout get'n scalped, being outnumbered, and while try'n to save our hides we have to run off and leave ever'thing we have."

The other men listened.

"Maybe we should go back and at least try and catch up with one of our other groups and either tag along with them or get them to come with us," Willy said. "Maybe even find us a good place to lay low for the winter and wait'll spring and join in a real wagon train goin' ta Californy. What'd ya'll think we should do?"

GH was the first to reply; "I'm with you on re-think'n this."

"We need to be better prepared for travel'n, an figger better where we're a go'n," G said.

Then Billy said, "Yeah, we took off without think'n this out."

Bill chimed in with, "I think we're all for looking at other ideas."

Then Willy said, "Okay, it's decided. In the morning we'll come up with something better. Let's sleep on it and go over it tomorrow."

The relief spread throughout and they nodded in agreement. Willy could see that the men were restored to their usual good humor. They stayed awake telling jokes and talking about home. Then they all climbed in their bunks for the night.

• • •

Next morning, they were having their morning coffee around the wood stove in the bunkhouse when

Willy started the conversation they'd all been thinking about.

"Okay fellas," he said. "What are you thinkin'?"

"I'm for go'n back to Independence and see'n what we can do about joining up with a wagon train take'n the Santa Fe Trail," G said. "At least we know it's passable."

"I'm with you," Bill said. "I want to be at least loaded with supplies wherever we go when we start out."

Willy spoke up. "I know there's two trails to get to Californy; the Santa Fe and the Oregon Trail. The Oregon Trail goes north to Wyoming then branches and you can go down through Nevada territory to Californy or up to Oregon then down. The other is the Santa Fe and it goes southwest, then due south through New Mexico territory almost to Mexico, then due west across the Arizona territory to what they call the Gila Trail, then into Californy. Any direction we take we need to prepare for trouble with Indians."

Billy, surprised by what he heard, spoke up, "Heck, I never knew you know'd so much about how to travel to Californy. Where'd you learn all that?"

Billy looked at Willy dumbfounded. Willy said, "I been ask'n round ever' time I went to town and saw people that looked like they was travel'n through, an' people in the saloon when I hear'd someone saying they'd been on one those trails."

GH jumped in with his opinion which sounded just like G's thoughts, "We should'na been so scared want'n to just get distance between us and the ranch. We should'a made us a real thought-out plan for this. What I think we need to do now is go back to Independence, get the supplies we'll need for a long trip and see iffen there ain't somebody else also going to where we want to go, so's we can join up an make us a bigger group to be safer. Least ways, we can find out more about the trails and really be prepared for this, not like we are now."

"Okay fellas," Willy said. "Looks like we're all think'n the same way, so let's get packed back up and head to Kansas City, since it's closer than Independence. It probably has a lot more supplies because the railroad goes to the City of Kansas in Missouri. Plus, they got three main travel trails coming out of there go'n west."

The men all rose and emptied their coffee cups. Then they turned and went to their bunks and grabbed what they had and went out to their wagons, put some grain in sacks for the horses and filled their water barrels. Heading back the way they had come was not an easy thing to accept. Neither was the fact they had lost so much time hoping to put distance between themselves and the Pinkertons. But Willy thought their new plan was better than heading into the unknown being as unprepared for the journey as they were. Passing through his thoughts were the other two groups. What had they run into? Were they finding out the hard way also that they should have thought things out better and been more prepared to confront this undertaking they had taken on? Probably not. They went to the big cities first and got their supplies. He regretted the choices his group had made and blamed himself mostly. But on the other side of it, he did figure they'd learnt a thing or two. Knowing there were Indians no matter which way they went was a good thing to know. And also, Willy knew that sometimes you have to do it one way to learn how to do it the right way. He was trying to feel a little better about it when G spoke up.

"When we get to the city," he said, "let's ask around about who has been over the routes and when the next groups are going to head out. If we can't find out anything that will help us right away, let's see iffen we can't catch up with the others who left the ranch, fore we just run in some direction away from where the Pinkertons might be look'n around."

Willy said, "Let's just get back to the city first, then worry about what to do when we're there. As long as we don't spend any of them gold coins, we should be all right for a time."

Seven days later they could make out the outlines of Kansas City far off in the distance. Their water was almost gone and food for their horses had been depleted to nothing the day before. They'd had to resort to stopping wherever they found a patch of ground that had some nourishment for the animals to let them eat. On the outskirts of town, they stopped at the first livery stable they came to that had stockpiles of feed. When they pulled up, a man came out and GH asked to board their animals for a week.

"Maybe longer," said Willy.

The owner was very happy to accommodate them. Taking the saddles off the horses they tossed them into the wagons on top of the tarps covering everything hoping that they'd keep the curious from trying to look under the tarp. Once the horses were situated, they went to the main street and looked up and down.

Willy saw a hotel not far from the stable.

"Right there, see?" He pointed, noticing that GH had to squint some. "Let's head that way. I'm starving," Willy said.

The men all grumbled about how empty their stomachs felt and together they walked up the main road and found the hotel. It had a big sign out front, "Sunset Hotel." They crossed the street and went inside to see about rooms. They all had a few dollars from the money Wiley had sent with them. Willy inquired about rooms for them and the young woman behind the counter near the lobby said, "Sure thing, gentlemen. How long you needin' 'em for?"

They all looked at Willy. "Well, ma'am that's an open question right now, but we'll know soon enough. How about we start out with a couple three nights."

She checked through her book, scratched out a few things, then said, "No problem. I got you down for three nights and we can change that whenever ya'll want to."

The men settled up, each of them pulling the money from their pockets and paying for themselves. After that was done, the woman said, "There's a bath house next door. Cost a dollar extra."

"That sounds fine," Willy said.

"You'll pay over at the bath house," she said.

Billy smiled at the young woman and she winked at him. He turned bright red.

Then Willy said, "After we've had a bath, let's meet in the dining room and work out what to do here."

They all agreed, seeming happy at the prospect of a good washing.

After ordering the baths, they had about a half hour to wait and were told of a general store right down the street where they could get some fresh clothes to wear while the ladies in the bathhouse washed what they had on. All five of them went across the street. In the store, Willy asked where they might find the telegraph, a wagon train company and the stage office.

The man running the place told him, "This is a big city. There's lots of places that will take you wherever you want to go. But be wary of anybody telling you they'll take you that ain't part of a regular stage outfit or wagon train traveling company. Make sure they got an office on the main street, that's where you'll find a telegraph office also. Those businesses on Main Street will be who you can trust. Anyone who's alone and offers to guide you, turn away.

After their baths they decided to just eat and go to bed. They would make their inquiries in the morning. Before he fell asleep, Willy thought about the ranch back home. He also pondered over the possible likelihood of running into the Pinkertons, who had the wrong idea about them stealing the Northern coffers.

That money was rightly theirs and most of it had gone to the church and the poor. He let his imagination carry him away for as long as he'd allow himself, about a good woman and a sturdy house where he could rest his body. He pictured himself working the land, being useful, and remaining free. He closed his eyes and in less than a minute he was out, snoring deeply.

CHAPTER 4

THE BIG CITY

The next morning, they saddled up and rode into the main city, marveling at how big the place was and how many people were moving about.

The town had been growing quickly, though not as fast as the City of Kansas in Missouri. The railroad had just arrived in the City of Kansas, Missouri which was the reason for the rapid growth. It was the furthest stop west on the railroad. It wouldn't be long before the bridge would be built to get across the river to Kansas City, Kansas and the last stop west on the railroad would be in Kansas.

The men found their bank on Main Street, went in and asked to have them communicate with the branch in Lawrence to get them $1,000.00 each. They'd each opened an account and deposited $3000; the money that Wiley had sent them all.

The bank manager gave them a look that made Willy feel the need to explain. "We need the outlay of cash to outfit ourselves for the trip we're planning."

"Sure enough," The manager said. "I'll do my best,

but it will probably take a few days, if not a week to get the funds authorized.

"I guess we got no choice but to wait," said Willy.

"Check back tomorrow," the bank manager said. "I'll let you know what I can do, if anything, to speed things up for you'ns."

Willy tipped his hat and gave the man a smile.

The men left the bank and continued on through the main street of the city looking for a wagon train outfit office or stage stop. Not finding either of those places in the near vicinity, they stopped at a saloon called Sonny's and ducked into the dark building.

Inside the smoke-filled room several people played cards around a table, and three or four were drinking whiskey at the bar. They went to the bar where G asked the bartender if he knew the whereabouts of a company that did wagon trains to California.

"The wagon trains are shut down till spring," he said.

"What about any guides with experience on the trails going to California?" asked GH.

The barkeep said, "There are a few men who are honest guides. The best one though would be Mountain Man Sam. But he's already heading west on the trail. I don't know where the other two are."

"You got names?" GH asked.

"Mountain Man Sam, like I told you, and Montana Mick and Dusty Trails. Montana Mick you might find around one of the boarding houses or the saloons near them, and Dusty Trails, if he's not got some filly down by the riverbank having a picnic or in one of the saloons, he's probably at one of the stage stops. Sometimes he goes down there looking for people to take out on the trails."

Before they left, Willy tipped his hat and thanked the barkeep.

Outside, the sun bright and the air cold, Willy said, "Okay men. Let's split up and start checking all the saloons and boarding houses."

The men silently broke into three groups and each went on their own way. A couple of hours went by when Willy walked into a saloon and asked the bartender about the men he was looking for. In that moment a man to his right spoke up.

"Who's looking for Dusty?"

"Well, I am. Name's Willy T. McCoy and am trying to get to Californy. We need someone to guide us who knows those trails and what we'll be up against."

The man said, "I'm a friend of Dusty's and I've helped him on a few trail rides. Where you staying? I'll see if I can find him and send him over to you."

Trying to size up the man, Willy said, "We're staying at the Sunset Hotel on the West end of town."

"Got it," said the man. "I'll find Dusty, and we'll go over there to that hotel."

The man finished his drink and went out the saloon door. Something about him. Willy couldn't put his finger on it. At that moment, the bartender leaned over to Willy and said, "Be careful around here. Not everybody's straight about what they tell you. I don't know the man that just left, but I've seen him around with some pretty shady characters. I do know Dusty, and I don't think Dusty would be friends with the likes of him. Just trying to look out fer ya, see'ns you'ns just got here an don't know nobody round these here parts."

Willy looked hard at the man to try and determine if he was being honest. He learned long ago that if the man talking to you was lying, he had a hard time looking you straight in the eye. The barkeep didn't flinch.

"Much obliged for the warning. I'll be careful." Willy tipped his hat and went outside to find the others and tell them what he'd learned.

Main Street was a long straight road, with many saloons and several boarding houses. Willy decided he would just walk up and down the storefronts until he found someone from the group. After about a half an hour he saw G coming out of a saloon and whistled to get his attention, then went across the street to meet him.

"Well, have you had any luck?" Willy asked.

"Not so far," G said. "It seems anybody that knows them knows that Mountain Man Sam is out guiding some folks and they haven't seen the other two."

"I think I have a lead on that Dusty Trails fella," Willy said. "I found someone that said they might be able to find him and send him over to our hotel. I'm going to go wait around at the hotel and see if I get lucky," Willy told him. "Iffen you see the others you can tell them that's where I'll be."

"Okay," G said. "I'll look around for them and if they don't have any news, I suppose we'll be headed over there to wait with you." G said.

Willy turned and walked towards the hotel while G started down Main Street looking for the others. Getting to the hotel, Willy took a seat out front in the chairs on the porch, hoping the man would have better luck than they did locating Dusty Trails. About an hour went by and the other McCoys showed up. None of them had any luck tracking down a guide. After standing around on the porch a couple of minutes, Bill said he would wait there on the porch with Willy, and the others could go up to their rooms if they wanted. Another hour passed. Then a man rode up and tied his horse at the front of the hotel and came up the steps. Willy recognized him as the man in the saloon he had talked to. Bill was looking at the man trying to size him up. He and Willy exchanged glances. Willy understood that Billy, like himself, didn't like the feeling he got or the looks of this character.

The man walked up to Willy. "Mr. McCoy, I found Dusty, but he can't come over right now."

"Oh yeah? Why's that?"

The man shuffled. "He said he would come by tomorrow morning and talk to you about guiding you. How many wagons and people are going to be in your group? And where exactly is it you're wanting to go?"

"We're want'n to go to Californy, but we could go to Denver City first, and then in the spring head down to Californy. Depending on how difficult and risky the road is to get there. We got five wagons and five men," Willy said.

The man's eyes lit up for a brief moment, and Willy got a bad feeling when he noticed the man appeared to be calculating something in his head. Willy did not like the looks of the smile that came over the man's face.

He looked at Willy and said, "That's not a very big group to be trying to travel across Indian country. Probably be a better idea to head for Denver City and from there join a larger group go'n in the spring over to California."

The two men nodded in unison. Then the man said, "Okay, then, I got what I needed. I'll let Dusty know. He'll probably be over sometime after breakfast."

That night the men discussed the meeting they'd had with the man and the possibility that he would bring Dusty the next day. They all wondered if the man was legitimate, especially after Willy told them what the bartender said. But they all agreed to wait and see if Dusty showed up. Then they all turned in early and slept.

The next morning after breakfast, all the McCoys were out on the front porch and two men rode up. They didn't get off their horses, but Willy and Bill recognized the man from the day before. The other man with him didn't seem to be very friendly. He gave off a hard exterior and sported a scraggly beard that ran down his face, almost to his chest.

The impression startled them, but they decided to listen. They all knew that a man had to take risks in life while guiding people through the mountains and Indian Territory. Willy reasoned that would make anyone have a hardened character.

The man spoke in a very deep voice. "I'm Dusty Trails. I hear you've been looking for a guide?"

Willy spoke up. "Actually, we're looking for some information and advice on traveling to Californy. We need to know if our wagons will make it and what our chances are of even making it alive?"

Willy's hesitation seemed to make the others cautious, too.

Dusty responded, "Wagons aren't a good way to get to California, unless they are pulled by oxen. From my experience the best way to go is using pack mules. That way no matter what kind of trails you run into you can keep going. Wagons can make it to Denver City or even Deadwood in the Dakota Territory. I've taken people to both places. You get to California by way of the Oregon Trail, going through Denver City. If you'ns are wanting to go the southern route or Santa Fe Trail to get there, chances are slim you make it no matter what you're using to travel. The Indians are real bad and unless you are in a big wagon train, I wouldn't advise it. Anyway, let's have a look at your wagons."

The McCoys looked at each other and shrugged their shoulders. There was an understanding between them and often they would agree or disagree just in the way they looked at one another, without having to say a word. Willy thought that Dusty Trails seemed to know what he was talking about.

They were all curious whether or not their wagons were sturdy enough to make this kind of a trip.

"We got them over across the street," Willy told the man.

He started down the steps to show the man, and the others followed him. The man took up the rear but never dismounted his horse. Reaching the livery, Willy stopped outside the fence and pointed to their wagons. The man claiming to be Dusty—Willy still didn't feel a hundred percent sure—would be able to know by looking at what they had if they'd make it from here. That is if he really was a guide. The man looked it over, saw that they were covered with tarps and had a pretty high cargo. Willy watched his expression, trying to figure out what he might have been thinking while looking at their cargo. The man looked at the McCoys and scowled, like he was judging them in some way. Either he wasn't sure they were hardy enough for the trip, or he was sizing them up; Willy couldn't tell.

He said, "I hope you have some room in there for food or you already have it in there, because you're looking at probably three weeks of traveling to Denver City and about the same if you went to Deadwood to wait out the winter."

"We'll have to talk about it between us where we decide to go," Willy said. His voice always soft and firm, grew even softer and firmer when he was trying to make a point. "Our end destination is still Californy for now. So, we need to make sure we have three weeks of supplies before we head out. I'm supposing that getting enough water won't be a problem going North or Northwest. How much are you charging to guide us?"

The man responded without batting an eye, "$250 each to take you to Denver City or Deadwood, paid the day we start on the trail."

Willy looked him directly in the eye trying to see if he was being honest, but he couldn't decide. "We'll talk it over between us. That's a lot of money. From what I hear the trail's pretty well marked from a lot of people traveling over the road to those places. We may just try to follow the roads ourselves. Where will I find you, if we decide to take you up on being a guide for us?"

"I'll come back in a day or two and you can let me know then. I have a place outside of town. It'll be easier for me just to come here and seein' as I need to be back here in a coupla days I'll check with you then."

He turned his horse and he and his partner rode back the way they came. As they were leaving, Willy turned to the others and said, "Doesn't seem very friendly and pretty short on manners."

Bill said, "Let's keep looking, see if we can't find that other fella and think this guy over in the meantime."

They all went back to the hotel. Willy worried. He never showed his worry, and no one could really tell, but he worried. He had a feeling the Pinkertons were probably looking for them. He wasn't sure he could trust this Dusty Trails, if he even was Dusty Trails. But just because a man might be short and rough didn't mean he was a cheater. Maybe you had to be a little rude and serious when you were a guide. The man did seem to know some things about the trail and the load that Willy and his group were carrying. But it seemed expensive. And there was still something about the man that made Willy nervous. He retired to his room and lay awake in the dark for a long time before falling asleep.

Chapter 5

The Stagecoach Inquiries

James was a religious man. He believed all the good that came into his life was on account of his faith. Everyone who met James saw this intelligence and kindness in his eyes. He was not one to talk about his faith or proselytize. He was old-fashioned that way. He kept it to himself.

His buddy, Festus, was a jokester. Not as smart as James but what he might have lacked in intellect he made up for in his loyalty and his easygoing nature. James and Festus, plus Jonesy and Junior, were distant kinfolk to those in the two other groups. They left the ranch the same day as the other groups and made good time to the City of Kansas. They were impressed by the bustling community and thought, for a city, it felt mostly friendly. Even though James did notice a few men who he'd stay clear of, he liked the place. You could get supplies and find a good place to rest for the night.

James, the natural leader of his group of Festus, Jonesy and Junior, suggested they pay the sheriff a visit to see if there was a good wagon train company worth their trust to take them to Deadwood.

They nodded in agreement. Festus scratched his head and said, "We should look into a guide, too. Also, what about us going to Ohio?"

James nodded. "We'll have to make some decisions."

James knew about the railroad and how it had recently arrived in the City of Kansas, Missouri. From what he could see, things were booming for businesses and trade to support the rapidly growing population of almost 4,000 people. The railroad still had yet to cross the Missouri river to the newly formed Kansas City, of the Kansas Territory, but the plans were in the works. Before getting to the sheriff's office, they saw the Central Overland California and Pike's Peak Express Company stage lines, one on each side of the street. James stopped his wagon and watched one of them pull over to his side and the other two crossing the street and pulling up in front of the other office.

Festus and James went into the Central Overland and Jonesy and Junior went into the Pikes Peak Express. When he walked through the door, James saw a rough looking man sitting at a desk.

"Hello mister," he said, "We're hoping to find a wagon train going to the Dakota Territory, or even a guide to show us the way. Know of any?"

The man smiled and said, "You're kinda late in the year to be go'n there, be freezing and two or three feet of snow by the time you got there. We don't have much call for any stages go'n that way till spring. Most ever'body stops here and waits out the winter, iffen they got any sense. There are a few fellers that take groups or wagon trains if the people insist on getting there this time of year, but they charge triple or more for a winter run, if they'll even take one."

James nodded as the man spoke. "We do have a couple of stagecoaches that will be go'n to Denver City this month, but that's it till spring unless something real important comes up."

"Well, where do we find these fellers?" Asked James.

"Either at the Bella Union Hotel or the Long Branch Saloon. Ask for Dusty Trails, Montana Mick, or Mountain Man Sam. Iffen they ain't there, just ask around. Don't really know where else you can find em."

"Much obliged mister, we'll get ta look'n," Festus said, as he and James turned back toward the street.

Jonesy and Junior heard basically the same answers from Pikes Peak Express. They were told the very same names to try and hunt down as guides. When they went back outside, Festus and James were waiting. After exchanging information, they looked around and saw the Bella Union Hotel. They walked to it and James went inside while the others waited on the boardwalk. As soon as he closed the door, he realized what kind of place it was.

He took off his hat as a lady came up to him and asked, "What's your pleasure mister?"

Smiling and turning red, he said, "I'm sorry, I thought this was a hotel for sleep'n. My mistake, ma'am."

He turned and walked back out. As he made it outside, the men waiting saw how red his face looked and started laughing. Festus managed to speak through his guffaws, "I guess you ain't never heard of the Bella Union, have ya?"

While James had been inside, Festus had explained to the others what kind of place it was and said to just wait for him to come out and see his face. They all had a good laugh at James, who they knew was sometimes inclined to spend an evening reading the Bible.

James pointed to a hotel down the street that had a hanging sign. "Café"

"Let's go try that one," he said. As they all started walking that way, Festus quipped, "I'll bet they have beds they'll let you sleep on."

All of them had to chuckle at that, even James whose good nature always helped him find a reason to laugh.

CHAPTER 6

KIN ARE NEVER VERY FAR

Roby, William and Tom made up the third and last group of McCoys who'd high-tailed it away from the ranch. When they arrived in Independence, they looked for signs on the storefronts advertising anything about travel westward, stage lines, wagon trains, overland guides west, hoping to find something to help them. Finding nothing of the sort, William suggested they stop at the nearby hotel with the sign by the door.

"Stage Stop" it read.

Inside, they found the place nice and clean. It had a dining room, so the three men decided to stop there and rent rooms for the night. After paying for the rooms, William asked the man at the desk, who called himself Charlie, about heading west.

"Do you know of any guides or wagon trains heading to Montana? We're want'n to head out that a way, only don't know nutt'n bout the place or how to get there."

Charlie smiled and replied, "Think'n on be'n pioneers are ya? Well, I can't tell ya much, ain't never been out that a way myself. But I bet someone down at the Overland Stage can, or at least, point you in the right direction to get the information you'll need. They're down the road heading out of town 'bout a mile. They got information on wagon trains and guides along with their own stage runs. The man that runs it is a good, honest fellow. Tell him, Charlie at the Moonlight Hotel sent ya over. He'll be glad to tell you'ns what yer up against."

William thanked the man, "Much obliged for the help. We'll just head on over there right now."

"We start serving dinner at five, so's you'ns got about an hour or so, iffen youse hungry," said Charlie.

"Thanks," replied Roby, "We are hungry. We'll be here."

They rode down to the stage office, William in front. William was a big man completely free of vanity or selfishness. He liked to read, and was so good at it, that he used to like to sit with the young'uns back home and teach them their letters. He was known to be patient, but if he felt himself wronged, you didn't want to be the one to receive his anger. Of the three of them, he was the best shot, the fastest runner, and the smartest.

Inside the stage office, they found a man sitting behind a desk reading the daily newspaper. He looked up as the door opened and put down his paper.

"What can I help you gents with?" he asked.

Tom spoke up. "We were told by Charlie at the Moonlight Hotel to come here to get information on traveling west. We need to know what's the best and safest way for us with wagons to get to Montana?"

"Charlie told ya that did he?" He said, smiling. "He thinks I know everything about go'n west. I can give you a map, recommend an outfit going in the spring wagon train, even give you the name of a guide, or two. But you'll have to talk to them about what to expect and what to bring on a trip like that. Unless you want to leave most of your stuff and take the stage."

"No, we need to take all our things and can't do without any of it," Roby said.

William watched and listened carefully. He knew that getting as far from the ranch as possible, in the quickest way was important. He also wanted to make sure they were safe, and that they didn't get into a bad way with any characters of doubtful quality.

"Well, the best man is not here, an he won't be back for a few weeks. He's taken a group to Denver City, in the Colorado Territory. Another that comes to mind, I haven't seen around lately either. Can't think of any others I know well enough to recommend. You could ask around town, see if he's around."

"Okay, what's his name and what's the name of the best one you talked about?" William asked, sounding a little disappointed at hearing they weren't around.

The man looked down at his desk, clearly searching his memory trying to recall the names of the men. After a long pause, he looked up and said, "The best one is Mountain Man Sam, goes by exactly that. Dusty Trails,

I'd say, might be a good second choice. He might be over in the City of Kansas. Oh yeah, there's another, Montana Mick, on account he's Irish and claims he was born and raised in Montana. If he's around, you'll find him between the Bluebell Boarding House and one of the many saloons up and down the street from there."

"Okay, thanks for the help. I guess we'll try to find them," William said.

When they exited into the waning evening, William said, "This is great; the one that's good is already guiding some people, the next best one's over in City of Kansas, and the other is a bar tramp and bordello hopper. Looks like we're start'n out this one hold'n deuces."

The other two looked at William, then both of them shook their heads, laughing.

• • •

James, and his group of McCoys had taken four days with their wagons to get to the City of Kansas, Missouri. But now, they were not finding any information about who could help them for the trip to the Dakota Territory, other than the names of three guides who were nowhere to be found. Having been in town for almost a week they were thinking they should go over to Kansas City, Kansas, and see if they could find one of the two guides that were supposed to be still around. On the 10th day after leaving the ranch they headed over to Kansas City, Kansas. Coming in from the east side of the city they stopped at the first decent looking hotel. After getting rooms and asking around about the guides, they decided they would just start from their end of Main Street and check every place that might be able to give them some information. They figured they would traverse the entire town end to end.

Being in no real hurry, they spent the better part of two days and were only a little over halfway through town. They had no idea that one of the other groups of McCoys—Willy, Bill, Billy, G and GH—were already on the West End of town.

Meanwhile, James and Festus learned that the safe and capable wagon trains would not travel until after winter was over. The only guides that anyone seemed to know about were the same three they'd been alerted to in the City of Kansas. Jonesy and Junior were just as disappointed. Back at the hotel that night, the four men spoke among themselves and the sense of discouragement was obvious.

Junior said, "From the looks of things, maybe it's best for us to find a place to rent and just stay here till spring when we can join in on the wagon train headed to the Dakota Territory."

Jonesy said he was thinking the same way, and added, "I think tomorrow I'll start checking on what places might be available to rent."

James and Festus said they would keep looking until they got to the end of the town in hopes of finding one of the three guides.

The next day as James and Festus asked around about the guides, one bartender told them, "There was another group of gents here just yesterday asking about those guides, might be a good idea if you tried to join up with them to travel, be safer that's for sure."

"You know where their stay'n?" James asked.

The bartender thought a moment, "You know I think I recollect hearing the man say they were at the Sunset Hotel at the West End the town. I think he even said his name was Willy McCoy."

Festus's eyes widened like globes hearing the name and James gave Festus a warning tap on his boot. Festus realized not to say anything or give his own name. James was relieved. He didn't want to give anyone anything to remember in case somebody ever came asking.

"Thank you," said James. "We'll try to find this McCoy fellow."

They walked out of the saloon and headed west. As they started walking, Festus couldn't help being excited that maybe someone from the ranch was in town. James put his finger to his lips to let Festus know he should keep his voice down. Then in a low voice he said, "We don't need to let anyone know there's a bunch of McCoys here in town. Let's just see if we can find them and maybe put together some kind of a plan to travel together."

That said they started walking fast toward the hotel, excited and hopeful that they'd see some of their kin.

The street seemed endless. James couldn't even see the end. "Let's go get our horses," James said. "Who knows how far the street goes or how far out of town this hotel is, and we can tell the others what we've heard."

They stopped at their hotel, but the others weren't there, so Festus and James went to the livery and saddled up. By the time they got to the Sunset Hotel it was almost noon and there sitting on the front porch, were two of the McCoys from the ranch.

They rode right up to the front and spotted Willy and Billy. While still on their horses Junior said, "Boy they'll just let anyone stay at this hotel."

Willy squinted into the sun for a moment, then recognized their kin.

"Well, I'll be danged, if that ain't one of the cooks."

They stood up and walked to the steps as the others dismounted. When they reached the ground, they exchanged handshakes and hugs with smiles all around.

James said, "I hear you're looking for a guide, least that's the word around town."

Willy replied, "I think we found one called Dusty Trails. He's supposed to come by tomorrow and we'll let him know if we're going to use him or not."

Festus jumped into the conversation, "Yeah, we been told of three men that might guide people and that name was one of them. So where were you going to have him take you?"

"We been wanting to go to California," Billy said. "We got as far as Abilene thinking we would get our supplies there, but there was nothing there except three or four shacks. It's just a stage stop. So, we decided to head back here and stock up on our supplies before we started out again. Let's meet up for dinner that way everybody can be together, and we can talk about what plans we have."

James and Festus looked at each other smiling and shrugged their shoulders. "That sounds like a great idea," said James.

There's a good restaurant here in this hotel. Why don't we just have dinner here?" Said Willy.

"Good," said James. "I'm sure that'll be fine with the others. We'll just go back and let them know. Let's say about 5 o'clock?"

They all agreed, and James and Festus got back on their horses. Willy and Billy looked at each other and were smiling big smiles, happy to have rejoined with some of the group from the ranch. They were excited to tell the others the news.

• • •

That evening at the Sunset Hotel after they all had a good, hot dinner, they went outside on the porch so the smokers could fill their pipes. They talked about the situation and all of them agreed to go to the Dakota Territory for now, and when spring came, those who wanted to go to California would join up with someone going across the Oregon Trail.

They talked about the $250 each for the guide.

"Why don't you'ns pay for the five of you's and then we can follow behind. Then we could all split the total for the five…" Festus said. He seemed to be trying to calculate the amount.

Willy said, "$1,250.00 would be for the five us,

which between the nine of us would only be..." Willy paused looked up at the sky calculating, then said, "About $139 for each."

The men all nodded in agreement with the happy prospect of getting away.

"Be good to know you'll be behind us," Billy said.

"And we'd be sort of travelin' together." Junior said, lighting his pipe.

• • •

The following morning Dusty Trails showed up at the Sunset Hotel and it was agreed they would leave town in three days. He told them what supplies they would need. So now both groups had to stock up on supplies to be ready to go. On the third day they had all their wagons ready and were waiting when Dusty Trails showed up with three other riders.

"Them three's for lookouts, just in case we come acrost any Indians," Dusty Trails said, spitting juice from the tobacco wad in his mouth on the ground.

James waited down the street, out of sight, but close enough to watch so he could tell the others when they should move out and start following them. He saw Dusty hold out his hands, and his kin handing over the $250 each. James watched the man put the money in his saddle bag. Something in the way he looked at his two scouts rubbed him the wrong way but shortly after that, the group started down the road and out of town. James quickly mounted his horse and rode to the other end of town and told the others to get a move on because the other group had already started out on the trail. By the time they got to the other end of town,

James' group was about 3 miles behind. During the day James and his men traveled on the road behind the others. Sometimes he could make out the wagons, but other times they were lost in the dust or past the horizon.

Meanwhile, Dusty Trails told his group to keep at least 100 to 250 feet between wagons for safety while they were traveling, so they were not too close together to get caught in a bunch and not too far apart that they couldn't help each other if something happened. As darkness began to fall on the first day, they were riding through a large group of oak trees on both sides of the road. Where the trees ended, they could not tell. As the road curved in a large arc, shots rang out from the trees. Willy let out a call to his kin. He couldn't tell how many guns there were, during the first volley of bullets because whoever it was, all of them had fired very close to the same time. One thing that was clear to him; this ambush had been well thought out and they had probably done it before in the same spot. Willy and Billy rode up to Bill, G, and GH, who were laying on their sides on the driver's benches in the lead three wagons. All three were hit with several bullets each.

Dusty and his men acted like they were trying to defend the wagons shooting in the trees. Willy and Billy both saw that they seemed to be aiming way too high or whoever had been shooting at them, had actually climbed into the trees.

Dusty started yelling, "Turn your wagons around and get out of here."

So that's what they did as fast as they could.

Fortunately, there was enough room for them to get their wagons turned around and once they did, they started racing back down the way they had come. During the time they were turning around, a few bullets hit the wagons throwing wood splinters into the air. Busy whipping their horses, Billy and Willy weren't looking back. They kept going for almost a mile and realized no one was chasing them and they couldn't hear any more gunshots.

Knowing the other group should be just a short distance behind, they kept going hoping to run into them. Then they could all go back to the ambush spot together, bringing help. Reaching the other group, both Billy and Willy yelled, "Ambush, ambush, ambush."

Jonesy yelled back, "Where?"

"Back down the road about 2 miles, where the oak trees get real thick," yelled Billy.

"Three of our guys have been hit. We need to get there right away," said Willy.

They all started slapping the reins on their horse's backs yelling "He yaa!" Trying to get the most out of their animals. By the time they got to the ambush site all they found were the three McCoys—G, GH and Bill—each of whom had been shot dead. The wagons were gone and none of the riders or the guide were there. It was too dark to follow a trail. They tried being quiet hoping to hear wagons or horses, anything that would give them an idea about where to go. Jonesy and Junior tried following the road for a short distance but couldn't see well enough to tell if the wagons had turned off and were hiding in the trees or had kept going, so they came back to the others who were standing over the bodies of their kin.

Feeling terrible, James said to no one in particular, "I knew we should have gotten closer as it got darker. I had a feeling something was funny about those guys."

Willy, who was devastated by the loss of the three men he had brought into the group, shook his head like he was trying to drain it of anger and sadness. "There's nothing more we can do tonight. Let's just wait here till morning when we can see if there's a trail to follow."

They all agreed and went about the somber task of carrying their brethren out of the way of the trail. They laid them side-by-side and covered them with blankets. They pulled their wagons in a circle around them and posted two guards, switching off throughout the night.

In the morning, as soon as they could see well enough, they got on the trail. They followed the road for about a mile at which point they saw tracks indicating that the wagons had turned off. Following that for a little distance they found out that it was a dead end. They had doubled back over their tracks and continued down the road. Apparently, only one wagon had acted as decoy, while the others kept moving down the road pushing their horses as hard as they could. They found a couple of other places where this had happened, which made the going slow because they had to check out every possibility. After about 20 miles, they found their horses dead alongside the road. They must have had other horses waiting and switched them out. That would have meant they'd likely placed the horses there a day or two before because the horses they rode would be too tired to pull wagons after traveling that far at that pace.

The men realized this had been planned. And likely by the so-called guides, none of whom were dead along the road or anywhere to be found. They'd been conned. At nightfall, they decided it would be best to go back and pick up the bodies of their kinfolk and go back to Kansas City, find the Sheriff and bury their family members. The next morning, they headed back, picking up the bodies and placing them in the wagons. It was almost nightfall the following day when they rode back into Kansas City. They stopped in front of the Sheriff's office. He had just come back from his dinner at the hotel next door and was about to close the office, when they walked in. They introduced themselves.

"Good evening fellas, I'm Sheriff Dodd, what can I do for you?"

Willy explained what had happened, while the sheriff looked at them in disbelief. They showed him the bodies and he shook his head in disgust.

He asked, "So you say this man is called Dusty Trails; that he was the organizer and guide of your caravan? What did he look like?"

Willy answered, "Well, he was about as tall as I am, heavier than me by 20 pounds at least, and had a scraggly beard almost to the middle of his chest."

The Sheriff looked at him and answered, "Can't be Dusty trails, I know him and he ain't got no beard, never has had one. Says it don't do good to have one out there in all that dirt and dust or in a fight."

"All I know is I met a man in the saloon here in town that said he knew Dusty and that's the man he brought to me claiming to be Dusty Trails," answered Willy.

"He must've been part of the group that has been robbing people around these parts over this last year. About every couple of months, a small group or single-family traveling west has been robbed. Most of them were killed and we found them alongside the road."

"I had hoped they'd moved on, but apparently not. It seems like they're just waitin' for the next travelers to happen along so that they can rob 'em."

Willy and Billy looked at each other. The other men remained quiet. All of them had their hats off. The Sheriff looked the wagon that contained the dead men.

"We best be getting these men over to the undertaker and tomorrow I'll try to get together a posse and we'll go see what we can find."

"Thank you, Sheriff," said James.

"You're welcome to come along. It would help us identify them if we come up to somebody."

James, who often grew quiet when he was angry or upset, answered for all of them, "Just say when and where, we'll all be there."

"Then I'll see you after breakfast tomorrow, around seven, right here," responded the Sheriff. Willy could tell the sheriff felt bad that this had happened on his watch.

They all rode, in a ragged unplanned procession, to

the undertaker, with James and Willy in the lead, both men staying quiet and looking only ahead of them.

"It's gonna take a couple of days to build the coffins and then y'all can have yer funeral," the undertaker said.

After all the preparations were made to bury their kin, the McCoys rode back to the Sunset Hotel and got rooms. They said nothing to each other as they turned in. Willy couldn't sleep. All he could do was pray and see his kin, G, GH ad Billy, lying there on the cold hard ground, their supplies long gone, including the gold coins they each carried. He felt responsible, even if the others told him he wasn't. Nothing they could say would make him think otherwise. That sleepless night, he could only think back on the mistakes he made from the moment they left the ranch and ask forgiveness.

Meanwhile, the sheriff went around to several saloons recruiting members for the posse in the morning. At 7 a.m. the men all stood in front of the Sheriff's office. Willy, Billy, James, Festus, Junior and Jonesy were among them. When the sheriff came out, the men all mounted their horses and took off. They headed down towards the ambush site. Since they were traveling without wagons, they were able to move much faster than the wagons had a couple days before. They made it to the ambush site by 1 p.m.

Looking around, they deduced that the wagons had stayed on the road and so they started following the tracks. They made it to the dead horses. At that point, since it was getting dark, they decided to make camp about half a mile further down the road. The next morning, they were moving at a fairly quick pace when they came to a crossroads and they couldn't tell which way the wagons had gone. It appeared that some wagons went in each direction. They decided to split up and one group went to the west, the other went south.

"We'll follow the wagon tracks for two days. If you come up empty, head back and we will all meet back up here on the fourth day," said the sheriff.

The men all nodded their heads and took off. Willy and his men eventually lost the tracks and didn't know which way they'd gone. Same for the other teams. At the end of the fourth day, they were all at the crossroads. The men were all very disappointed that they couldn't find out where the wagons had gone. In defeat, they headed back to Kansas City.

Once there, the McCoy men broke off and went to the undertakers.

"Sorry, men," said the undertaker, taking off his hat. "I built the coffins but couldn't wait any longer. Had to bury them in the town cemetery."

He took the men to the cemetery and pointed out the graves. The McCoys were then left to themselves. They gathered around the gravesites and all of them took their hats off and bowed their heads.

Willy was the first to speak, taking a step forward, "I want you boys to know I feel really bad about what's happened to ya. I blame myself for believing that guy really was Dusty Trails and I wish I could make it up to you. I'm sorry to say that the best I can do is to live for you, because we couldn't find those bushwhackers. Maybe we still might run across their trails somehow and I hope we do, but until then I will try my best to let you live through me. I know you've gone to a better place, where you don't have to look over your shoulder anymore and can rest in peace. You'll be sorely missed. Please forgive me for get'n you killed."

He stepped back into the group and James stepped forward. Holding his hat in his hands belt high, he said, "Everyone should know that there's nothing to forgive and it wasn't Willy's fault. We all went along with what we were doing. Just because Willy happened to find the man, doesn't mean it's his fault because we all decided to go with him. We just want you to know that we did our best and hope that you can rest in peace, amen."

They all followed with their own "amen" and silently walked back toward their horses. Mounting up, Jonesy asked the others if anyone wanted to keep asking around about guides. They decided they would check around again tomorrow to see if any of the real guides had come back into town. Theirs was a very somber group. They decided to put their horses up in the livery and all go back to the same hotel for the night.

• • •

The next morning, they split up and started checking again for the guides. By noon they had covered most of the Main Street saloons and the hotels but heard nothing about the guides. No one had seen any of the three of them. By the end of the day, they had covered the entire town and returned back to the hotel. During dinner they discussed their options.

"Why don't we just form our own group and follow the map we got from the stage office," said Jonsey. "The route must be pretty well marked from the other travelers who've gone over it."

"Yeah," agreed Junior. "I'm thinkin' we don't need to hire a guide. Why risk more problems from dishonest people?"

"Might be a good idea to just stay the winter here in Kansas City," James, ever the level-headed one said.

"Me and Billy went by the land offices and we have information on a couple of ranches that people have given up on. They're available to rent or buy," said Willy.

"We done the same thing," said Festus. "Junior came with me."

Junior nodded his head, chewing on the bite he'd just taken. The others were almost finished with dinner, all ready for dessert.

"Well, then," said James. "Why don't we go take a look at the places that're available."

"And then," Willy chimed in, "we can decide if we want to travel or stay for the winter." Only two men remained of the group of five McCoys that had originally wanted to go to California and both of them—Willy and Billy—were of a mind to stay the winter in Kansas City.

"Plus," said Billy. "Here is exactly where we ran into those killers and they might just come back."

Willy and Billy exchanged glances. Willy believed that Billy was probably thinking the same thing as he was thinking himself. It was not likely that they'd ever see those thieves and killers again once they found the gold in the wagons. But you never knew.

Festus and James sat back in their seats. Junior and Jonesy looked undecided. But after they'd made inquiries at the land offices, they'd found ten ranches to look at and decided they might as well check them out.

The men, feeling settled for now, enjoyed their custard pies, and later went out on the veranda, buttoned against the cold wind, enjoying a pipe. They were even able to laugh a little, cracking jokes amongst themselves about their naivety in what they were trying to do. By the time the moon rose high overhead, they were all exhausted and a little sad about their lost kin, the lost gold and their waylaid dreams. They went back in the hotel where they retired for the night.

During the next couple of days, they were able to take a look at all of the ranches for rent and sale. They found a couple of nice ones. On one of them, the owners had been killed. At another, a young couple had lived there, but when the husband died, the wife went back home to her parents with her son. The ranches were in fairly good shape. Some of them needed a little bit of fixing up; the ranch houses, the barns and corrals but for the most part, they seemed like they'd be livable at least for the winter.

Now they had to decide what they were going to do to pass the time, at least for the next few months.

CHAPTER 7

DUSTY TRAILS

After spending the better part of a week in Independence hoping one of those guides might show up or news of their whereabouts would come to them, Roby, William and Tom decided they might try going to the City of Kansas to look for the guides there. None of them had shown up and they were getting bored waiting around. They packed up and rode to their destination with no idea that their kin, both groups, were across the river in Kansas City and just about to sign a contract to rent a ranch for the winter.

• • •

The McCoys already in Kansas City decided which ranch they wanted to rent to wait out the winter. They also hoped that the killers might just show back up. They picked out a nice ranch that already had a solid bunkhouse for ranch hands, a couple of out buildings and a big old farmhouse where they could easily sleep. There was a good well for water, and the buildings needed few repairs. They started fixing the place up and one day, needing supplies, Willy and Festus went into town. There, they ran into Sheriff Dodd, who told them he had seen Dusty Trails the day before coming out of the Bella Union.

Willy and Festus decided they would return to town and look for him after they dropped off the supplies they had picked up for the ranch. Later that day when they got back to town they went straight to the Bella Union and asked for Dusty. The hostess there told them that Dusty would be at the Doubletree Hotel if anyone was looking for him. Finding out from her where the hotel was, they headed straight over.

Once at the hotel, the desk clerk pointed to a man in the dining room.

"That's your man right over there."

They approached a young man, rugged from the outdoors, clean shaven just like the sheriff had told them, and probably under 30 years old. He was eating a hearty dinner of fried chicken, grits and some overcooked root vegetables of unknown origin which he'd pushed to the side.

"Good evening, Mister," Willy said politely. "I hear you may be a man named Dusty Trails who can guide people to Deadwood in the Dakota Territory or over to Denver City in the Colorado Territory?"

The man stopped eating and looked up. He brought a napkin to his face and wiped. After swallowing the food he'd been chewing he said, in a hearty voice, "Yep, that's me, who's asking?"

"My name's Willy T. McCoy, and me and my kinfolk are trying to get to Deadwood or Denver City before winter sets in too hard."

Dusty looked him in the eye and said, "Well which is it, Deadwood or Denver City? Cuz it's two different directions."

"We haven't decided which yet, but it won't take long for us to decide," replied Willy.

"I just came back from Deadwood and snows getting' pretty deep and temperatures are freezing go'n into the Dakota Territory, don't know iffen I want to be making another trip till spring. I think going to Denver City would be worse about now since it's higher up in the mountains, so I'm kind of inclined to take a break till spring, but I'd be glad to take you then," he said.

Hearing his answer deflated their aspirations of getting further away before spring. Festus spoke up, "I think our group would be willing to pay extra if you are inclined to do it."

Dusty looked at him and said, "Have you fellas eaten yet? Why don't you have a seat and maybe I can explain things a little better."

The waitress, who'd been keeping an eye on them, spotted Dusty motioning her over.

"Kathy would you please set these fellas up with a couple plates of today's special, thank you kindly."

After they sat down, he went into describing the dangers of traveling in the winter that were added to the many dangers that existed in the summertime.

"I'd rather risk my neck and your neck when the weather is warm. If we went now, I'd worry about freezing to death. It wouldn't be too hard to find ourselves stuck in a bitter cold snowstorm."

The men listened carefully. It was good to hear about the realities from someone who seemed truthful.

Looking back and forth between the two of them, Dusty said, "It gets cold enough down here, but at least you can get out of it going inside somewhere. Out on the trail ain't many places you can get out of that cold. I have done winter trips before and I charge four times normal rate, but I think this winter is going to be tougher than most and I don't want to risk my hide out there, let alone yours."

At that moment the plates of food arrived, and the waitress told them to enjoy the meal. Finishing his, Dusty winked at the waitress who was very pretty with her long blonde hair and those blue eyes. "Kathy," he said, "You still got any of that delicious apple pie I ate yesterday?"

She smiled and replied, "Yes sir, coming right up. I'll be right back with it."

Breathing in the aroma of their hot meal, the two men realized how hungry they were and dug in. They also got a piece of pie for themselves. When they were finished, they all rose together from the table. Dusty reached out to shake their hands saying, "It's a pleasure to meet you gents, the meal is on me, and if you still want to go in the spring, I can put you down for my first trip, but I think that's best for all of us."

They shook his hand. "Thank you for the meal, Mr. Trails," said Willy.

"We'll be back in touch," Billy said. "Will you be at the hotel?"

Dusty replied, "Whenever I'm in town, this is where I stay. If they don't burn it down, I'll be here."

"Okay, we'll be back to find you."

The men left and returned to the ranch to tell the others what they had learned.

CHAPTER 8

UNEXPECTED KIN

It took Roby, William and Tom, four days to get to the City of Kansas. They spent almost an entire day of just waiting for their turn at the ferry, because of the backup of people waiting to be ferried across the river. Coming in from the east side of the city they were on the far side of town, eight miles from the ranch their kin had rented.

After getting storage for their wagons and settling into their hotel, they did what the others had done; rode down Main Street and checked all of the hotels, saloons and any stage or wagon train travel office they could find asking about the guides. Around noon time they came upon the Doubletree Hotel, deciding they would have lunch there. Not expecting any information on the whereabouts of the guides they still asked at the front desk if anyone knew who they were and how to find them.

"Dusty Trails is staying there, but I haven't seen him," said the hotel clerk.

Excited at the thought that they found one of the

guides, they agreed to have lunch there and wait for him to show up. They were almost finished with lunch when a man came up to their table and said the desk clerk told him they were looking for Dusty Trails.

"Well sirs, I am Dusty Trails. What can I do you fer?"

Tom spoke up, "Well Mr. Trails, we're hoping to get to Montana, and we think we need to get us a guide, cuz we never been that a way."

Dusty went about explaining the same thing he had told the others the night before about waiting till spring. He did say that he expected Mountain Man Sam to be back in the next couple of weeks and they could check with him.

"He might be willing to brave the elements," Dusty said. "But as far as I'm concerned, I'm closed till spring. I do have a group that wants to go to Deadwood in the Dakota Territory as soon as spring gets here. You might want to hook up with them, it's always better if we have a bigger group. Makes things a lot safer."

Roby asked, "Do you know where we can find these people?"

Dusty replied, "Can't say as I can. I didn't ask them where they was stay'n. I do remember though the man told me his name was Willy T. McCoy."

At the sound of that name all of them smiled and looked at each other. Roby was about to tell him that that was their kinfolk when he noticed William give a slight shake of his head, so instead he said, "I think we need to start looking around town for this fella. Much obliged for the information. And consider us part of that first spring trip of yours if this other feller can't be found."

"Will do," said Dusty.

The McCoys thanked Dusty for the information, each shaking his hand then turned and went out the door. Outside as they were walking away, Roby said, "Well, I'll be. Can you believe that one? Willy McCoy and the other four who left with him for California, stopped, just like us by the snow."

The other two laughed. "We got to find them," said Tom.

William nodded in agreement.

For the rest of the day, the three men checked for the other guides and asked about Willy McCoy. Not finding any information about the people they were looking for they went back to their hotel.

The next day, they used horses because the town, to their surprise, was a little too big for walking when they were looking for people. While scouring the town once again, they ran into Sheriff Dodd who told them about that other group of men that had in mind to go to the Dakota Territory.

"Be careful though, men. Your friends got mixed up with thieves and killers. Three of 'em were killed, and they lost three wagons."

"Are you sure about that?" William asked. It was like a dark cloud crossed overhead.

"Yes sir. Those men are buried right over in the town cemetery."

The three men looked at each other with worried glances. "So do you have any idea where they're staying?" William asked.

"No sir, I do not. But I do know they rented a ranch to wait till spring afore they try again. I'd say check with one of the land offices. There's only three in town. Someone there might be able to tell you something. But remember what I said; be careful about hiring a guide and if you do, make sure they are who they say they are by asking around town."

"Yes sir," said Roby. "We met a guide named Dusty Trails. Tall man, nice guy. Shaggy hair but no beard. Stays at the Doubletree?"

"That's probably him. Did he tell you he'd wait for spring?"

"Yes," William said.

"Then that's probably him. No trail guide in their right mind would take anyone this time of year."

They decided to quit searching for the guides and find the land offices in the hopes that they would locate their kinfolk. It took only two tries. The second place they went into was the one that had rented the ranch to Willy.

"They're our friends," said Tom. "We've worked a ranch together."

"We wanted to stop in and pay them a visit," said William.

"Okay, then." The man looked into a file and pulled out a sheet of paper with all kinds of writing on it. He then said, "It's on this side of town. Just go about five miles that way," the man pointed, "and you'll see it down a small road with two giant oak trees on either side. You keep on that road, and you'll run into the ranch.

The men thanked him, and they mounted up, feeling happy about going to see their kin while heading out of town towards the ranch.

Coming down the entrance to the ranch they saw one man chopping wood, one man with a bucket at the well and one out in the corral feeding the horses. Stopping at the hitching rail in front of the house, they saw Willy and Billy exiting the house. When they caught eyes, both men broke into wide grins.

Willy yelled out, "Hey everybody, come see what the cat drug in!"

Everyone within earshot hurried over to see who was there. After handshakes and hugs all around, the McCoys went inside the house. They all got some refreshments, coffee mostly and some leftover biscuits staying warm on the stove.

"We heard from the sheriff what happened. We were sorry to hear that," Tom said. He shook his head. It was so quiet with everyone reflecting on the tragedy

Willy said, "Yeah, dagg nabbit, I blame myself every day for G, GH, and Bill. It's hard to believe they're not with us anymore and those scoundrels got away with it."

"We sure as heck won't fall for something like that again," William said. "Now that we're all together we got us a good-sized group, almost what you'd call a wagon train with just us."

Willy wanted to change the subject away from the ambush and the deaths. "We should all set out together come spring," he said.

Festus said. "That's a good idea except we don't all want to go to the same place. We could all go to Deadwood and then those of us who want to continue on to Montana or California can do so if we didn't like what we found in Deadwood."

James added, "Well, we have a lot of time between now and spring to decide what we think is best. For now, I think we need to set up the bunkhouse, so they'll be room for everybody to stay here; that is iffen they want to."

The men all spoke at the same time. It was clear they all wanted to stay together.

"Well then," said Festus, "let's get out there and see what needs do'n. We all just been bedding down in the house. C'mon let's go have a look."

The men went out to the bunkhouse to get it ready for people to sleep in. While looking over the bunkhouse, William suggested that they all hide their gold somewhere out on the ranch so that in case someone came snooping around, they wouldn't find it in the barn where they had it covered with tarps.

They all agreed it was a good idea and the next day they all took their boxes out to various places on the property and buried them, making mental notes of exactly where they were. Then feeling good to be reunited, the men put on a big dinner that night, and enjoyed the company, talking about home and expressing their sadness for all the McCoys who'd passed before them.

CHAPTER 9

BIG JOHN

The man who impersonated Dusty Trails was known to the gang as "Big John." He and his band traveled more than 50 miles before they stopped to check the wagons they stole from the McCoys. There were nine men that made up the band of ruffians. They pulled back the tarps and started rifling through the things they found, announcing what the items as they were moving things around. One of them said it seemed like they had all the same stuff in each wagon. One of them got to the large crate up towards the front on one of the wagons, opened it up and pulled out the blankets that were on top. There they saw the three strong boxes underneath.

"Hey, hey, what do we have here?" He said. As he tried to lift it out, he realized how heavy it was and called for help, "I can't lift this. Someone needs to help me," he said.

Another man climbed up on the wagon and between the two of them they struggled to get it out of the crate. He pulled out his pistol and shot the lock, then opened the latch. Once the top came up, they saw the bags with the drawstrings. He reached in and pulled one free with some difficulty. He loosened the drawstring and stuck his hand inside feeling the coins. He pulled out a handful and let out a yell, "Hot damn! We hit the mother lode! Them boys were loaded down with gold. Look at this! These here are $50 gold pieces. There must be $10,000 or more just in this bag."

All of the men let out whistles of disbelief.

Big John said, "Okay everyone, looks like we need to divide up what we've got."

One of the other men spoke up, "Let's just make sure all three wagons have the same amount and three of us will keep one wagon to divide between us. That gives us all the same share."

They checked the other wagons making sure they all had three strong boxes, opened them up and counted the bags. They decided that each wagon had the same contents. They would all get equal shares.

"We need to split up and go our separate ways," Big John said. "Looks like we don't need to do any more robbing for the rest of our days. What we need to do is get as far away from here as we can and start living a new life."

They put the coins back in the wagons the way they had been and pulled the tarp back over each. As they started down the road the men talked among themselves about what they were going to do with their share.

Big John, a surly man who spoke little except to get business done, listened to the other men.

One of them said, "I'm goin' back home to Arkansas and buy me a ranch."

Two of the men said they would join him.

Another said, "I'm going to St. Louis."

Two men joined in and said they wanted to head that way too.

Big John, and his two friends kept mum. The two men with Big John knew about his temper. It didn't take much to set him off. And when he got mad, it was like a dark cloud hung over him and followed him wherever he went.

After five days of traveling together, the bandits came to a crossroads indicating St. Louis in one direction and Arkansas in another. This was where they parted ways with two wagons going in the direction of St. Louis and one wagon heading towards Arkansas. None of them knew that the Pinkertons were tracking those gold coins.

When they reached Glasgow the two groups heading to St. Louis decided to separate and one wagon continued on towards St. Louis. The other contained Big John and his partner, known as "Slim" and a man named Hank. Slim was the man who had introduced the McCoys to Big John. Big John and Slim decided to put their shares on pack mules. They didn't need the wagon anymore, so they let Hank take the wagon. Slim and Big John put their shares on the mules they bought in Glasgow, using one mule for provisions and two mules for their gold. The wagon headed south and the two men with three mules each, headed east, taking their time because by now they figured no one was chasing them.

By this time the Pinkertons were spread out halfway across the southern part of Missouri following the stories they'd heard of men spending gold coins. The information was mostly collected from the towns that had the telegraph as a means of communication. So far, they had only been able to see the coins that were spent, not the people spending them because the men stayed in town for just a day or two. By the time the Pinkertons arrived they were long gone.

At least they had confirmation that these were the coins they were looking for, so they continued following every lead that came in. About a month had passed since the Pinkertons left the McCoy Ranch and headed out to follow the trail of spent gold coins. They learned that a single coin was spent in Glasgow to purchase six mules, pack saddles and cargo harnessing. The leader of the Pinkertons sent word to the other agents to meet him in Jefferson City. He thought it was strange that only one coin was spent and that it was so far north. All the other trails to follow started out in southern Missouri and were heading northeast. A week later all the Pinkertons met up in Jefferson City.

When the Pinkertons started out on their mission there were ten of them. The youngest and newest recruit was killed trying to capture some men who were spending gold coins, so now there were nine of them. The leader was Agent Tucker. His eight remaining deputies were, Will, Cody, Jared, Thaddeus, Dale, Jim, Jake and Art.

Agent Tucker was smart and often testy. Raised in the North by wealthy parents, he was the oldest of four siblings. Since he was a young boy, he wanted nothing more than to win. At everything. He made winning his motto and he set about to win at cards, in sports and later, at catching criminals. He was educated at the best schools and then, to his mother's dismay, he left home after college to find out what he was interested in instead of settling down and having a family. When he landed a job with the Pinkertons, he became known as a natural leader. And a strategic tracker. He held his head high—a little too high—and to some it seemed like he did it because he was making up a few inches in height. He wasn't a particularly nice person, but he wasn't a mean person either. He lived for the work he did and was only satisfied when justice was done.

"Okay, men," he said. "We're going to split into three groups."

The eight men sat still and attentive, waiting for their assignments.

"Will, Cody and Jared, you'll go to the nearest towns due south of Glasgow until you reach Columbia."

The three men nodded.

"I'm putting Cody in charge," Tucker said.

"Yes sir," said Cody. Cody had just turned 23 and had a sweetheart back home. They were planning to get married in the summer. Cody was a good tracker and was known as someone who had strong common sense.

The second group consisted of Thaddeus, Dale and Jim. "You three will go directly west across Missouri then down to Clinton and stop there."

"Yes sir," they said at the same time.

"I want you to try heading off the men who have the coins before they get as far as Clinton." He ordered this since no news had come to Jefferson City where they were.

"They're either avoiding the bigger cities or just haven't made it to us yet. Hopefully they're trying to take the shortest route south."

The three men nodded and said, "Yes sir." It was no surprise when he put Thaddeus in charge because after Agent Tucker, he was the smartest of the lot.

Tucker looked at the last two men and said, "Jake and Art, you're with me. We'll head northeast to Kingdom City."

Tucker decided that if they came up empty his group would head over to St. Louis which was directly east of Glasgow. This way they would travel along the routes where they knew the coins were being spent. If any news came from any towns, they would get communication about them in their destination cities and make a new plan from there.

"None of you are to go further than your assigned city without communicating with me first in Kingdom City. Eventually, if we haven't found them, we will combine the information we've all gathered and figure out which direction to go from there."

The men stood up, looking serious. They understood their missions.

CHAPTER 10

WAITING OUT THE WINTER

The McCoys decided they had no choice but to wait out the winter in Kansas City. So far Mountain Man Sam had not returned, and he was their only hope of getting to Deadwood during the winter, unless they wanted to try on their own to brave the elements and confront the dangers of an unknown trail. A week passed, and one day while in town Willy saw the sheriff leaving a cafe.

"Hello, Mr. McCoy," the sheriff said.

"Howdy, Sheriff?"

"Glad I ran into you."

"Oh yeah?"

"I knew you was lookin' for Mountain Man Sam, and I wanted to let you know he's back."

"Do you know where he's stayin'?"

"Yes, I do. He's at the Bluebonnet Hotel."

"Thank you, Sheriff," Willy said.

Willy watched the sheriff walk away down the dusty road. A high, cold wind was coming off the plains and he buttoned up. He thought for a moment whether he should go back to the ranch and gather one of the boys or go straight to see the guide. He decided that now was the time to pay Mountain Man Sam a visit. The man had been so hard to find, Willy couldn't be sure a chance like this would show itself again. So, he headed over to the Bluebonnet. He walked inside the warm hotel and asked the man at the desk if he knew where Mountain Man Sam was.

"He was here this morning," the desk clerk said. "But I saw him leave and I don't know where he went."

"Okay," Willy said, disappointed.

"He's usually here for supper."

Willy tipped his hat and thanked the man for his help.

He headed back to the ranch. When he arrived, everyone seemed restless. The repairs needed were already done so they could live there. They had a lot of time and they didn't have much to do other than the daily chores: getting water and feed to the horses and feeding themselves. None of the McCoys liked sitting around—they needed to be doing something.

Willy gathered them all and told him that Mountain Man Sam had been seen in town and that they could probably catch him at supper time if anyone still wanted to attempt the trip this winter. The men began to talk at once.

But James rose above the others. "It's too cold and we don't want to risk our lives freezing to death," he said. "Like Dusty Trails said, I think it would be better to wait till spring."

But Roby, William and Tom, who wanted to get to Montana, said they were willing to brave the elements if Mountain Man Sam was willing to take them up there.

"I'll go into town and try to catch him at the Bluebonnet at supper time," William said. "And hear him out."

At 4 o'clock in the afternoon William got ready to go to town. The wind was blowing, and the air was cold. As he was saddling his horse, he decided he would have his supper there at the Bluebonnet whether he found Sam or not. He took off into the evening, the cold settling into his bones. Once he arrived, he tied his horse up and went inside the hotel. Dinner smells filled the air. A waitress brought William to a table and he asked her to bring him some coffee for now, that he was waiting for Mountain Man Sam.

"I don't know him," William said, "Is he here, by any chance."

She looked around the room. "No sir, but he eats supper here ever night."

"Would you be so kind as to point him out if you know who he is," William asked.

"I'd be happy to," She said. She smiled, "It won't be hard to miss him, because like his name, Mountain Man Sam, is a big mountain of a man.

"Thank you kindly," William said.

He didn't have long to wait. A few minutes later a giant of a man walked into the dining room. He wore a bearskin coat and toted a knife on his belt that must've been more than a foot-long and 5 or 6 inches wide. The man sat at a table by himself, and the waitress went over to him, took his order and pointed out William. Sam nodded across the room at him, so William stood up and went to the guide's table.

"You must be Mountain Man Sam."

"That's me," Sam said.

"Name's William. I've been told I should talk to you about someone to guide my group to Deadwood."

Sam looked at him, and William was sure Sam was trying to decide if he was some kind of criminal trying to escape something or maybe someone who had gold fever and wanted to get up into the gold territory. When it seemed like Sam decided that William was neither, he said, "Tell me what you're thinking. This time of year, the guide'n fee would be high. There are lots of dangers any time, but in the winter, you also run the risk of dyin' from the cold.

William nodded. He was still standing beside the table, his hat in his hand.

"Have you et yet? Iffen not, have a seat," Sam said.

William said, "Thank you, no I haven't, and my stomach's been growling for the last half hour smelling those good smells comin' from the kitchen."

As he sat down Sam asked him, "Why are you so insistent about getting there in the wintertime? Are you running from something?"

"Naw. We was waiting for spring but my kin and me can't stand sit'n around doing nothing wait'n for warm weather."

Sam looked him in the eye and William could see

that the man believed him "Iffen you want to get there at all, we'll have to leave right away because coming back just now I was running into better'n a foot of snow and by the time we get back up there we'll be looking at 2 feet of snow. Maybe more."

William nodded his head.

Sam said, "I wasn't going to take another trip and don't really want to, but if the price is right, I might make an exception."

"What's the right price?"

Sam leaned back in his chair and said, "In good weather I'll do it for $250 a head. But now the way things are, it'll cost you $1000 each. Otherwise wait till spring and I'll do it for $250 each."

"Wow, that's a big difference. Don't know if we can come up with that much," William said. In fact, he knew that the price wasn't a problem, but for safety reasons, he didn't want anyone knowing they had a lot of money.

"That price is due to wintertime; the robbers and the Indians are more desperate, not to mention the weather makes it a lot harder to travel and survive," Sam answered quickly. "Seein' as I'm responsible for your well-being and my own, I got to buy extra supplies and take a bigger risk."

"Okay," William said. "I know how much you want. But I'll have to go back and talk it over with my kinfolk."

"Understood."

"But for now, let's just have us a good supper."

Mountain Man Sam nodded his head, obviously eager to eat. Luckily for both of them, the waitress arrived shortly with heaping plates of good, hot food.

While they were eating Sam said, "Why do you want to go to Deadwood anyway?"

William put his fork down, and said, "Well, me and my kinfolk have been ranch hands for the last year and a half since the war ended, and we thought we were pretty lucky to come out of the war alive and in one piece, and most of us saved all our money; which doesn't amount to much when all is said and done. Still, we thought we'd see if we could get lucky and find some gold up there."

"You know, there's been a couple of good strikes up there, but they've pretty much petered out now and most folks are leaving because they're not find'n any more," Sam said, chewing his food.

William shrugged it off, and replied, "Even if we don't find any gold, we want to explore some of this new territory. Maybe we get lucky, maybe we don't. At least we'll have seen some new places and maybe find us a place to settle down and make our own ranches. Leave the bad times far behind us."

"I get that," Sam said.

After they finished their supper, the peach cobbler arrived. The canned peaches had been harvested locally and still tasted excellent.

When all the food was gone, Sam leaned back and smoked his pipe. Both men were quiet. After a time, William said, "Well, thank you. I'll be heading back to the ranch now."

"Thanks for the company," Sam said.

"I'll let you know what my kin folk think they want to do." William said. "Are you going to be staying here for a little while?"

"Unless we take the trip, I'll be here till spring," Sam said.

"All right then, I'll be in touch either way. Thanks for the information and the company for supper."

When he got back to the ranch, the night had grown cold. A biting wind made it feel colder and William tucked his head in his coat as he walked into the warm farmhouse. Tom and Roby were anxious to hear what he'd learned. He told them what Sam had said about costs. When Roby heard the price for a winter guide, he whistled but said nothing.

"A good night's sleep will allow us the time to ponder over this and more energy to pack what we need iffen we're gonna get ready for the road," William said.

The men nodded in agreement and together they decided they would sleep on it and make their decision in the morning.

Chapter 11

Risk

The next morning over coffee, they talked and decided they wanted to risk a winter trip to get away to Deadwood. They were going stir crazy just sitting around. And they wanted, originally, to get far away from the Pinkertons with their gold and their freedom intact. So, when the sun came up, William rode back to town and found Sam finishing up his breakfast at the hotel.

"Mornin,'" Sam said.

William told Sam that they wanted to go through with it. "Even though it will eat up almost all the money we saved."

Sam told him what they were going to need as far as clothing and supplies. "And I mean it when I say it, get extra food and supplies. Extra blankets, extra cured meat, flour, beans and fatback. Get some extra warm clothes and potatoes, anything you can find."

"Okay," said William.

"I can't stress it enough, you got that. Extras."

William nodded. "Got it."

"Let me know as soon as you're ready and I'll take a look at what ya'll have to make sure you're prepared," Sam said.

William hurried back to the ranch and passed along the information to Roby and Tom, and they made plans to go into town the next day and get all the supplies they were going to need. After that the men spent the day at the ranch getting ready.

Early the next morning, William, Roby and Tom had breakfast with the others and told them what their plans were. William could see that some of them thought he was out of his mind for taking on such a risk. They were quiet on the way to town. William wondered if this was a good idea. But they'd committed and he didn't want to place any doubts on the others. Once they arrived in town, they took time to get the supplies that Mountain Man Sam had told them to get. Then, after they finished their shopping, the three men rode to the hotel and told Sam they were ready for him to come check out their gear.

Sam came outside in his bear skin coat to take a look and he met Roby and Tom.

"It might be a good idea," Sam said, "if you can afford it, to pick up five or six mules apiece, because I don't know how bad the snow's gonna be and the wagons might not be able to make it."

William said, "We'll check around and see if we can get the animals, and we'll let you know when we do, iffen we do."

The next day they scoured the town's livery

stables and managed to come up with six mules apiece and the packing harnesses, so Tom notified Sam that they were ready.

"I'll need to be paid at the start," Sam said. "We'll leave tomorrow morning after breakfast."

"Where do you want to meet?" Tom asked.

"Just bring your wagons and mules to the front of the hotel and we'll leave from here." Sam said.

The next morning, the three McCoys said goodbye to their kin. It was a somber moment. William was thinking that it was possible they might never see their kin again. He could tell they were worried about the three of them taking off in the middle of winter. The mood was subdued as the three of them got on their horses and rode away. It was early when they arrived, and they had breakfast with Sam in the hotel. In the lobby before exiting the hotel Sam wanted payment, so they each gave him $1000 from what they'd had wired from Lawrence.

Tom, William, Roby and Sam started their journey to Deadwood.

• • •

The Pinkerton agents, Will, Cody and Jared made it to Columbia in three days. The second group of agents, Thaddeus, Dale and Jim stopped in a couple of small towns on their way to Clinton. One of the towns was called Tipton, where they decided to stay the night after a couple hard, cold days on the trail. The third group, Jake, Art and the head agent, Tucker, made it to Kingdom City on the end of their fifth day. They had stopped for the night in both Fulton and New Bloomfield.

Stopping only for a few hours twice before reaching Columbia, Cody, Will and Jared paid a visit to the Sheriff's office. Cody introduced himself and the men shook hands.

"How can I help you?" the sheriff asked.

"We're looking to see if anyone has come through these parts, spending fifty-dollar gold coins," Cody said.

"Whose asking," the sheriff said.

The men pulled out their papers identifying them as Pinkertons.

"We've been tracking stolen gold coins being spent all over southern Missouri, and we aim to find ever one of these Varmints," Cody said. He was a man who did not have patience for people who made excuses or dawdled on the job. He aimed to have Tucker's job one day, and to marry his sweetheart back home.

"No one notified me of anything like that, but I'm happy to put the word out around town," said the sheriff.

"Thank you," Cody said.

The other men nodded their heads.

The second group, Dale, Thaddeus and Jim, decided to rest up in Tipton. Like the other group, the three men in the second group found the Sheriff.

After their introductions, Thaddeus said, "Just wondering if anyone has been spending any cold coins around here."

The sheriff didn't ask any questions. He just

scratched his head and said, "Don't know about any gold coins, but there was a man come through by himself in a wagon. He's staying at the only hotel in town."

The sheriff gave the three men directions to the hotel, and they rode over there. Inside the hotel, they approached the desk clerk, who looked a little nervous as the three men drew near.

Thaddeus took off his hat. He had a tangle of red hair, which matched his beard and mustache. "We hear there's a new arrival in town. Just wondering where he's from and how he's paying for his room."

The man's eyebrows raised as he said, "He gave me a fifty-dollar gold piece to hold while he stayed here."

The clerk did a fairly good job of describing the man and told Thaddeus that the man had gone down the street to the livery stable for his wagon and horses.

Not wanting to waste time, the three men, with Thaddeus in the lead, hurried over to the livery stable, and told the owner what they were looking for. He showed them which wagon had come in. So, they now had to find the man somewhere in town. They headed towards one of the two saloons in town. Entering the first saloon, they looked around and saw a card game going on. Thaddeus was the first to notice that one of the men had a small stack of $50 gold pieces in front of him. Then the other two noticed and they decided to walk over and meet the man.

But as they drew near, the man's eyes opened wide. He'd been spotted. He was clearly nervous at the sight of the badges on the lapels of their coats. Not realizing that the Pinkertons had been searching for the gold coins, the man was sure these lawmen had followed the trail from the ambush site where they took the wagons.

Thaddeus whispered, "Let's get around him," but the three men didn't have time to surround him before the man jumped up and pulled his pistol out. While trying to pull it back and out of the holster and swing it upwards his hand hit his chair behind him, and his gun barrel caught on his own holster forcing him to redirect his aim. This gave the agents just enough time to get their guns out and fire before he was able to. Three bullets hit the man and as he fell, he pulled the trigger on his pistol sending a bullet shooting wildly and out through a wall. One of the townspeople ran for the sheriff.

The sheriff was a tough man who'd been around a long time and when he saw the mess in the saloon, he said, "I thought you boys were detectives. Don't you know enough to take a look inside before walking in and heading straight up to the man you're looking for? You could've killed some innocent people. Heck, I'm just a small-town sheriff but I know enough to wait till they come outside before confronting them. That's just plain common sense for us."

The men said nothing. Thaddeus felt like a fool. It was his fault. He *should* have known better.

"At least there's a couple of witnesses that say he drew first," the sheriff said. "Otherwise, we'd have a problem."

The sheriff told one of the men standing around—a restaurant worker from the hotel dining room—to fetch the undertaker. Looking hard at the agents, he said, "Maybe you ought to go check out his room and his belongings to see if you can get any information or find more of this gold since he's not alive to talk about it."

The sheriff asked a couple of other bystanders to help him get the body over to the undertaker's place and, muttering to himself, he said, "I never saw any lawmen so dumb…don't even know how to approach a suspect."

• • •

Thaddeus was embarrassed. For being such a smart man, he sure made a dumb mistake. Still standing there, they looked at each other and Thaddeus said, "Come on, let's go look over his stuff."

He couldn't stop thinking about how it was his responsibility and now he had made all of them the laughingstock. He vowed to himself it wouldn't happen again. They rode to the hotel and checked the man's room but all they found were some extra clothes and a saddlebag. They went back to the livery and through the contents of the wagon. There they found the strongbox full of bags of gold. Taking the gold over to the sheriff's office, they asked him to contact the general.

"He will send someone to pick up the gold," said Thaddeus.

He decided it would be best for them to keep moving towards Clinton, as they had made as big a spectacle of themselves as they possibly could. They were all too embarrassed to hang around town and hear all the talk about how they didn't know how to do their jobs. They argued about what had happened for a while, until Thaddeus couldn't stand it anymore and took all the blame just to shut them up. Then they mounted up and headed towards Clinton.

"We'll notify Agent Tucker once we get there," Thaddeus said. Then he rode on ahead of the other two detectives hoping not to speak to them for a while.

CHAPTER 12

BORDELLOS AND CARD TABLES

When Will, Cody and Jared got to Columbia, they paid for some rooms in a hotel, deciding to keep an eye on the saloons and general stores, while hoping they would hear from the sheriff that someone had come to town and spent a gold coin or two. They had been there a day and a half when the sheriff rode over to their hotel and asked for Cody at the front desk.

Cody joined the sheriff in the hotel lobby after rousing the other two.

"A wagon with three men accompanying it rolled into town. They stopped at a livery and headed over to the nearest hotel. The clerk over there said the three men were arguing between themselves about not having any money. They disappeared for a few minutes, in the direction of the livery. When they came back, one of them pulled a gold coin out of his pocket."

Cody nodded. His two partners stood beside him.

"I have it on good authority that the three men plan on staying there at least a couple of days, assuming that no one is following them," the sheriff said.

Will nodded his head.

"From what I understand," the sheriff said, "they paid the livery stable with their change from the hotel and divided up the rest, so they all had some regular money. Then they headed over to the saloon."

Although the sheriff didn't know where they were at that moment, at least the three Pinkertons knew there were three men in town that had spent a gold piece. Now they had to find them and try to get some answers out of them, without having a shoot-out.

Cody looked at his men. "You ready?" he said. "We ought to head over there before they disappear."

The other men agreed, and they headed over to the hotel.

What Cody, Will and Jared didn't know was that after having a couple of drinks, the three men decided to get a bath and a shave and then head out on the town to see if there were any willing fillies around town somewhere, even if they had to pay for it. After freshening up, two of them went to a boarding house and found themselves a couple of women to go upstairs with.

The third one went to a saloon that had rooms upstairs where the ladies working the saloon would take their customers. While all three were enjoying the company of the ladies, Cody and his men split up to try to locate the men as quickly as possible and agreed they would meet back at the Sheriff's office in one hour, hoping they would have the information they needed.

They went door to door to all the saloons, boarding

houses and brothels, discreetly inquiring whether there were some new faces that had come in recently. When the hour was over, they had located all three men, who were not very far from the hotel where they were staying. One of the men was alone at a saloon.

Meeting back at the Sheriff's office they went over the information they had about the whereabouts of the men. They also had the layout of each place so they could do some planning. They decided it would be best to take on the man in the saloon who was by himself first, hoping they might be able to overpower him, or convince him it was useless to put up a fight.

Inside the saloon the bartender told them that the man was with Katie in the last room on the right.

"Any way he can get out if he knows we're coming."

The bartender said, "Since there's only one floor above, there's a chance the man could try to jump out the window."

"I'll take the alley, just give me a minute to get there," Cody said.

Will and Jared waited exactly one minute and then headed up the stairs. Reaching the end of the hallway, Jarrett motioned Will with a finger to his lips to keep quiet while he listened at the door.

They could both hear a woman's voice saying, "Wow, where'd you get all of them gold coins? You give me one of them and you can stay here a week with me!"

The man responded, "Sure darling, I'll let you have one, but I don't think I'll be staying here a week. But you might be get'n a week's worth of work in a couple of days outta me."

She replied, "That's some big talk you're gonna have to back up, sweetie." She giggled saying, "Okay, give it here."

Jared heard the woman say, "Help me with this corset", then boots being pulled off and a gun belt dropping to the floor. He heard the woman giggle once more and then footsteps and the creaking of the bed as she climbed in.

• • •

Inside the room, not yet aware that the Pinkertons had him surrounded, the man took off his long johns and said, "Let me in there, and I'm not talking about just the bed."

It was at that moment he heard the floor outside the room creak. The man in the bed looked at the doorknob just as it started to turn. It was locked, so the door didn't open, to the frustration of the agents. Realizing what was happening, that someone was trying to get into his room and catch him off guard, he jumped out of the bed and grabbed his long johns, pants and gun belt. His first thought was that he was about to be robbed. He reached for his boots and was set to grab them and put them on when he heard the words "Pinkerton detectives, We're come'n in."

When he heard that, he dove headfirst out the window, landing in a heap on the ground and losing his grip on his belongings, except for his gun belt. He landed hard, but not hard enough to stop him from quickly trying to gather his stuff and hightail it out of there. While reaching for his pants he heard someone say, "Hold it right there, put your hands up!"

He turned in the direction of the voice and pulled his pistol from the gun belt. Cody, seeing the pistol come free of the gun belt, had no choice: If he let the scoundrel raise his pistol, he could be a dead man. He fired quickly and hit the man in the middle of his chest flopping him over onto his back, where he gave one convulsive jerk and was still, his life gone from his body. Cody went to the man and checked his pockets. He found three gold coins and some folding money. He then took the pants and draped them over the man covering him as best as the pants could. Within seconds Jared and Will were at his side looking down on the dead man.

Cody looked at the other two and said, "Well, I hope it goes better with the other two then it did here."

They told one of the bystanders that had come out to see what the commotion was about, to find the sheriff and tell him what had just happened. Then they headed down to the boarding house to confront the other two. Going inside, they were greeted by a lady fancifully dressed, saying; "Hello gentlemen, what's your pleasure today?"

Cody smiled, and said, "Sorry to disappoint you ma'am, but we're here on different business. We're looking for two men who came in here a couple hours ago and we need to talk to them." He flashed the badge on his coat, and she understood.

"Please sir, I can't afford to have any gunplay, or my girls or customers getting hurt. Is there any way you can wait till they come outside?"

He thought about that, and about what had just happened down the street.

"Unfortunately, ma'am, we don't know what they look like. But I understand your predicament. If you can tell us which rooms they're in, we can do this in their rooms,"

She didn't seem too happy about that. "What happens if you end up in a gun battle in the room? Anyone in the next three rooms could take a bullet. No, no, we can't have that. What I can do is, when they leave, I'll come outside and signal you or you can wait here in our getting- acquainted salon, and when they come down, I will let you know who they are. Then you can confront them outside. Does that sound reasonable?"

Cody thought it over a moment, "Okay, we can do that. That's probably best for all concerned and probably the safest."

He looked at Will and Jared and told them to take off their coats and hide their badges, so as not to panic the men when they came downstairs. They settled in and spread out all around the getting-acquainted salon. A couple men came in and sat with a couple of ladies, then disappeared up the stairs. Otherwise, everything was quiet. After an hour had gone by, Cody was getting restless and tired of waiting.

He walked up to the woman in charge. "I'm sorry, but just how long do you expect us to wait? Those boys could stay in there for days."

"No, they won't," she said. "We don't allow more

than four hours at a time, and most of the time the men come back down within two hours. So please just have a little more patience, I'm sure it won't be long now. Let me get you some fresh coffee, I'll be right back."

Almost as soon as the lady disappeared from view, they heard voices and footsteps on the stairs. A man and a woman reached the bottom of the stairs. The man complimented the lady on the fine time he had and put his hat on heading for the door. When the man exited, Cody ran quickly to find the lady and told Jared, "Keep an eye on him and see where he goes, but don't let him know you're watching him."

Once he found the madam, they ran outside but saw nothing. Cody searched for Jared and found him leaning against a support post for the overhead walkway in front of the saloon. Jared motioned with his head indicating that the man had gone inside the saloon. Cody asked the woman to come and identify whether this was their man.

They hurried over to the saloon and Cody said, "Let's walk by slowly and casually, like we're just taking a stroll and talking. You just try to glance inside and see if you recognize him, but don't make it obvious you're searching inside for someone. Okay, let's go."

He put her arm in the crook of his elbow, so it seemed he was just escorting her on a leisurely walk. As they passed the windows and the double swinging doors she looked inside while they continued on walking past the saloon.

"Well, was it him?" Cody asked.

She looked at him, and he could tell by her expression that she felt bad. "I'm sorry," she said. "That's one of our regulars, those two must still be inside."

Frustrated at his situation Cody said, "Let's get back over there before something else happens."

As they walked back, the sheriff, who had been dealing with the body of the man Cody had shot hurried over to them. He tipped his hat to the lady and said hello to Cody.

"We got two men inside," Cody told the sheriff. "We know they've been using the gold coins. We don't want a repeat of what happened back there, so we're trying to keep it safe."

"If you don't want to just sit around and wait, I can post one of my deputies across the street to watch the front door," the sheriff said.

"No, that's okay Sheriff, I think that's going to be a little too obvious. One of them could look out a window and realize you're watching the front. Since they don't know us, we're probably the best chance."

"I understand," the sheriff said.

"I'm going to have Jared over there sit on the boardwalk, a little ways down the street and the other two of us will just wait inside."

"Okay, suit yourself, just so you're careful and you don't get any civilians hurt trying to apprehend those two. My deputies are dealing with the last situation. A lot of people running scared, so don't get reckless," the sheriff said.

Cody left it up to the sheriff to walk the lady back to

her business and went to talk to Jared.

"All right, now listen carefully," Cody said.

"Yes sir," Jared said.

Cody thought maybe he was being sarcastic since in reality they were of equal rank. But he let it go. He liked Jared who was younger than him and maybe even tougher.

"Wait down the street and keep an eye on the front of the boarding house," Cody said. "Then if we get into a situation, I want you to use your judgement. We want to catch these guys with no bullets flying if we can."

Jared nodded. "Got it," he said and left for his post.

Walking toward the boarding house, Cody noticed that the two floors above the entrance had walk-around balconies that went all the way around the building. He walked back inside the boarding house and took a seat in the getting-acquainted salon. He hadn't been seated but five minutes when a man came down the stairs. The madam was standing at the reception podium.

She turned towards the stairs and smiled. "Hello sir, I hope everything was to your liking," she said.

He smiled back, and said, "Just fine ma'am. I'll be back later or tomorrow for sure."

He put on his hat as he walked out the door and she nodded to Cody indicating that was one of the men they were looking for. Once the man was outside, Cody told Will, "One of us needs to stay inside and make sure the other one doesn't come down while we go after this one."

"Okay, I'll wait here," replied Will.

Cody quickly exited and started in the direction the

man had taken. He was about 30 yards behind the man when he saw Jared coming across the street to head the man off. As Jared walked toward them, the man started angling his steps toward the other side of the street. Jared didn't miss a beat and continued crossing the street like he was out on a casual walk.

Cody crossed too as Jared walked towards the man. In moments, Jared was in front of the man in the middle of the street. Jared called out, "Excuse me Mr., can I talk to you for a minute?"

Immediately, Cody realized that the man knew they were lawmen. He saw the man go for his gun. So did Jared. In his haste, the man's shot went wild, but Jared's shot did not. He hit the man in the shoulder. The impact turned the man and he saw Cody. He was holding his shoulder as he tried to raise his pistol towards Cody. That was the last movement he was conscious of, as Cody fired quickly, knocking the man off his feet. They rushed over to see if he was going to live, but turning him over, they spotted the blank stare of death in the man's eyes. Realizing the gunshots might have alerted the other man, they turned their attention back to the boarding house.

• • •

Rufus Purdy was on the second floor with his lady when he heard gunshots. Looking out his window he saw the scene in the street where his partner lay sprawled out on the ground. He watched as two men, one whose badge glinted in the cold sunlight, ran toward the entrance of the boarding house. He quickly grabbed his clothes and pulled them on while his mind was racing to think of a way out and wondering how they got caught.

The lady in the bed said, "What's your hurry?"

He flicked her a gold coin and said, "Gotta run, Miss. You sure are a pretty lady."

Looking outside, he decided to check the balcony—maybe he could jump across to the next building. He ran around to the side farthest away from the street and seeing that the distance was not far to the next building he thought he could jump from the railing on the balcony and make it to the next one. Launching himself in the air he came down on the sloped roof of the next building and scrambled up over the roof to the other side hoping to get out of sight quickly. Hearing the shots from the street, Will, who had been at the bottom of the stairs decided he'd better go up. The woman who had been in the man's room was running down the stairs.

"Where is he?" Cody yelled at the woman.

She never stopped running as she draped a shawl around shoulders and yelled back, "Third door on the left." She ran so fast that in seconds she was gone from sight.

He took the stairs two at a time and charged through the third door on the left, finding the room empty and the doorway to the balcony wide-open. He ran out, looked in both directions and saw nothing. Then he heard a crash, and saw the man landing on the next building's roof. He tried to yell for Will and Jared, but they were already heading up the stairs on the inside of the bordello. In seconds, they were all in the room, and Will told the other two men what had happened. Cody told Jared to head for the livery stable because for sure the man was heading there for his horse.

Jared took off and reached the street in seconds. He ran towards the livery. Cody and Will were right behind him.

"Will, you go that way, I'll take it this way," Cody yelled already turning right. They each ran off in opposite directions around the building next door. Not seeing the man stealthily moving on the roof, they started cautiously moving around the buildings towards the livery checking around every angle before they moved into the open space between buildings.

They were moving much slower than Jared because of the potential for an ambush. When Jared got to the livery, he saw movement in the stalls and someone trying to saddle a horse. He started moving cautiously in the direction of the stalls keeping behind anything he could use as cover. He made it to the end of a wagon parked outside the stalls. By then the man had finished saddling his horse. The man looked around, and not seeing anyone, (Jared was well hidden), he decided he had time to gather up some of the gold hidden in the wagon. Jared could see the entire thing. He pulled his horse toward the far end of the stalls where there was a gate that he unlatched. He let go of the reins and went through one of the stalls to a wagon that was just outside. Climbing up on the wagon he looked around, and not seeing any movement he bent over and opened up the crate with the strongbox inside. He grabbed one bag in each hand. When he did that, Jared stood up and called out, "Just keep your hands where they are!"

The man realized he was at a disadvantage, because he had a bag of gold in each hand and his gun in his holster. But probably because he couldn't bear the thought of going to jail, he opened his hands letting the bags fall and bent his knees, so he dropped at the same time that he was reaching for his pistol. By the time the pistol came out the man was almost squatting. When Jared fired, the sound was probably the last thing the man ever heard. Jared fired thinking he would hit him center mass, but when the man squatted, the bullet hit him square in the forehead, knocking him backwards and sprawled out over the driver's seat of the wagon.

Will and Cody heard the gunshot and sprinted to the livery stable. There they saw Jared walking towards a wagon where they could see a pair of boots sticking up in the air over the driver's seat. They checked the wagon and found the gold, placing the two bags the man had taken out, on top of the strongbox.

The sheriff and his deputy were hiding out in the general store closest to where the boarding house entrance was and witnessed the gun battle in the street. They followed the agents as they made their way to the livery stable. Being cautious before entering the stable, the sheriff called out, "Is it all clear? Are you all okay? Do you need a doctor?"

Cody responded, "No we're good. Can't say the same for those two guys we were trying to catch. Going to need the undertaker again."

They showed the sheriff the gold and told him how to contact the general so he could send someone to pick it up.

Cody took off his hat and wiped his forehead. Even though the air was cold, he felt the sweat on his brow. The others did the same, shaking their heads.

"I guess we better send a telegram to Kingdom City and let Mr. Tucker know what we ran into and see what he wants us to do from here," said Cody.

Jared looked at his friend. Will was gathering up a few of the spilled coins and put them in one of the bags. "At least we caught him red-handed with the gold," Jared said, as he put them inside the strongbox.

Back at the hotel, Cody sent a telegram to Tucker, and asked for instructions. Now all they had to do was wait for the response. The men treated themselves to dinner and a rare libation, all of them happy to put the day's events behind them.

The other two groups were still traveling.

CHAPTER 13

BIG JOHN AND SLIM

The road was wide, and Thaddeus, Dale and Jim were riding abreast of each other on their way to Clinton. The winter was getting colder and deeper. They'd already had some snow. Thaddeus thought about his wife and newborn son at home. On the long days, whenever he was away from his small family, he would think about sitting in the parlor with his wife, as she held their sleeping baby. Some days he missed them too much. It was easy to drift into those thoughts while traveling but once there was action, he was focused. His best skill was his ability to recall every detail of every criminal, every crime, every arrest, and every shootout, right down to the clothes people wore, the way they walked and the details of their surroundings. His photographic memory was legendary.

Meanwhile, Tucker, Jake and Art were about five miles outside of Kingdom City. Tucker wondered how the others were doing, especially Cody, Jared and Will. They were probably already in Columbia. Tucker was a loyal man, a smart and strategic personality. He always worried to himself about his men. But he controlled himself in front of others so what they saw was a man they could lean on and trust, especially when things heated up. They moved on as the light of day rose, unaware that a telegram awaited them in the telegraph office ahead of their arrival.

• • •

Big John, the impersonator of Dusty Trails, and Slim, his partner who had made the introductions to the McCoys, had made it to Kingdom City the day before the Pinkertons. They believed they'd made an untraceable escape. Big John, who might have been the meanest and smartest of all of them, knew enough not to be spending gold coins as they traveled. He warned Slim not to spend any of his coins, because he was sure that the men they robbed weren't the original owners of those coins. Obviously, by the sheer number and value of them, the coins were stolen property.

He had the money that he had charged the McCoys to guide them to use while they traveled. Big John had divided up that money giving $500 to Slim and keeping $750 for himself. They decided they wanted to live it up a little after all their hard work and hard traveling, so they picked the best hotel in the city and got the best rooms they could find. They bought new clothes and pampered themselves with hot baths and fresh shaves. They took their meals at the best restaurants they could find.

As Agent Tucker and his group entered Kingdom City, Big John and Slim were enjoying themselves at the fanciest brothel in the city. Big John was taking his time with his lady. But Slim had tired of his lady's company and was looking for a high-stakes poker game. He found one in the brothel, where a local card shark had established residence.

The card shark, Allen Roberts, was one slick character. He would let players win for a little while, get their confidence, and then suck them in on hands he knew he would win. If he thought they were more than one-night players, he was known to even lose $1000 and goad the winners into coming back the next day for double the stakes claiming he wanted a chance to win his money back. When Slim set down at the table, Roberts told him the rules were table stakes. You could only play with what you had with you. A man could not make a bet for any more than he had on him. Slim, confident that he had plenty of money to play with said that was fine with him. After a couple of hours Slim was up $200 but he was getting tired.

"I'm gonna head out of here after the next three hands," he told Roberts. He noticed the man's sunken cheeks and black eyes.

"Sounds good," Roberts said. "You comin' back tomorrow?"

"Yes, I am," Slim said,

In the next three hands, Roberts reduced Slim's advantage to losing, to the point that he had only $100 of his own money.

Slim claimed he was tired and shouldn't have played those last three hands. He said, "I'll come back tomorrow when I've had some rest and we'll see how that turns out."

Upset with himself, he gathered up the money he had left and went back to the hotel, determined that the next day he would play a lot better and beat that man for all he had. Big John had long since returned to the hotel and was sleeping in his room. Slim decided sleep was the best thing for him to do as well.

The next morning, they both slept late, and it was almost 10 a.m. before they came out of their rooms. They ate breakfast in the hotel, and both felt well rested and ready to challenge the day. They first headed to the brothel.

"I reckon I'll be staying here all day," said Big John.

Slim laughed. He said, "I got to give somebody some payback at a card game."

"Well, watch yourself. Don't spend any of those coins, you here?"

"I won't need to. He's a bad player, far as I can see, and just got lucky takin' my money."

They both walked into the brothel.

"I just remembered somethin'," Slim said. "I'll be right back."

Big John shrugged his shoulders. "See ya later, then."

Big John found his favorite lady from the day before and disappeared up the stairs. Slim snuck back over to the livery stable and made sure no one was watching as he found the supply packs they had taken off the mules. Inside the stall area, he took a long look around to make sure no one was around, then he slipped a handful of gold coins in his pocket. In his mind, Big John was over-reacting. They'd made it this far, and no one had been spotted on their trail. It would be okay, just this one time. Besides, he wasn't all that sure the card player named Roberts was actually a bad player. He wanted to make sure he had the funds to win his money back and then some when he got the right cards. Putting everything back the way it was, he headed back to the brothel to find his card game and more importantly the player who he believed had stolen his money.

Slim found his gambler at the same table and sat down, taking out a handful of gold coins and setting them on the table in front of him.

Roberts, who was too cool to give away his surprise, said, "You came to play for real this time, did you!"

"You bet," Replied Slim, settling in his seat. A couple minutes passed, when Big John decided to go down and get a bottle of champagne for himself and the lady. Downstairs, he asked the Madam to get him a bottle of the house's best champagne.

"Sure thing," she said. "I'll be right back with it."

While waiting Big John noticed a sign indicating where the poker room was and decided to take a look. He couldn't believe his eyes when he saw Slim at the poker table with a stack of gold coins in front of him. Immediately angry, he went up to Slim and whispered in his ear, "You get your butt up and outside right now, I want to talk to you!"

They went outside the front and stood on the boardwalk.

Big John, trying to keep his voice low, but still full of anger, told Slim through clenched teeth, "You are the biggest idiot I have ever met. I told you not to spend any of those coins."

"I'm not spending any, I'm playing poker, I'm not buying anything," Slim said.

All Big John could do was shake his head and say, "When I told you not to spend any of those coins on anything, that meant don't let anyone see any of those coins. Well, you done ruined this town for us, and I can't take any more chances on an idiot like you. We part ways from here. You're on your own. I'm getting the heck out of here and you're not coming with me."

Slim stood there with his mouth open and watched Big John storm away heading towards their hotel. Slim thought to himself; *Well, what's done is done and I don't think it was that bad of a thing I did.* He never believed it would cause any problems. Slim couldn't resist the need to go back in and beat that player at poker, so back inside he went and sat down at the table.

Meanwhile, Big John went back to his room, grabbed his things and went back to the room at the brothel. The lovely lady was confused.

"Gotta run, little lady," Big John said.

"I'm not pretty enough for ya?"

He gave her a kiss and said, "You're too pretty, darlin'. But I got an emergency and have to run."

She made pouty lips, so he left her some cash, finished dressing, and hurried over to the livery stable saddling up his horse and gearing up the pack mules.

He was so angry, he felt like steam must be coming out of his ears. He grabbed his share of the coins and rode out of town in less than 20 minutes from when he saw Slim at the poker table, going in the direction of St. Louis.

The Madam who had gone after the champagne was looking around for Big John. She looked all over the ground floor and then went up to the room he had been in. Not finding him there, she went to look for him in the poker room, glad she hadn't opened the champagne. In the poker room she noticed the man she had seen Big John with the day before sitting at the playing table. Then she realized what was sitting in front of the man; two tall stacks of gold coins. At once, she felt nervous. Her heart started pounding. She tried to get out of the room without anyone noticing she was about to panic. She took the champagne back to the cellar and headed straight over to the sheriff. After telling the sheriff what she'd seen, he told her to go back and keep an eye on the man while he went after the Pinkerton agents.

At the hotel, the sheriff found agent Tucker having lunch.

"Mr. Tucker, you might want to postpone that lunch of yours," the sheriff said.

Tucker raised his napkin to his lips and patted them. "Why's that, Sheriff?"

"The madam at the brothel just came to me. She's seen someone, an average looking fellow in the card room with two stacks of gold coins piled up in front of him."

Tucker stood up immediately, taking a last quick bite of his meal, one final sip of his drink and said, "Thank you, Sheriff."

Then he took two stairs at a time on his way up to notify the other two who were in their rooms. If they were thinking they were going to take a nap, they would have to think again.

He burst into Jake's room first. Jake was reading the Gideons Bible from the nightstand and smoking a pipe.

"Apologies," Tucker said, looking at the ground. He hated to bother a man in his privacy. "But I just got word from the sheriff there's a man in the card room over at the bordello. He's got two stacks of gold coins in front of him, playing poker."

Jake jumped up and to Tucker's relief he was fully clothed.

"Go grab Art, next door, and meet me downstairs. You have less than a minute. We don't wanna lose this man."

"Yes sir," Jake said.

As Tucker headed back downstairs, he could hear Jake rousing Art, who sounded as if he'd just dozed off.

A minute later, Agent Tucker briefed them as they hurried over to the bordello. "We're going to walk in their real nonchalant and act like we're going to come up and sit down at the poker table."

His men watched him with serious expressions on their faces.

"I will be directly behind this feller and you two will go on his right and left, and when I nod my head, each one of you grab an arm and pull him out of his chair. He's not a big fellow so he shouldn't be that hard to grab."

"Yes sir," they said at the same time.

"And let me be clear," Tucker said. "I want to take this one alive."

They nodded and then the three men made their way to the poker room. Doing their best not to raise any suspicion, Jake and Art walked on either side of Slim, and Tucker went behind him. Slim felt the presence of someone and looked over his shoulders to see, but he thought it was just people wanting to see him play poker and turned back to the game. Agent Tucker nodded and Jake and Art grabbed Slim's arms up close to his armpits and pulled him upwards and over the back of the chair. In the process, the chair tipped over. Tucker quickly got in front of Slim.

"We're Pinkerton detectives and we've been on the trail of these here gold coins for quite some time. Now you're going to tell me where you got them."

Slim looked at him in surprise, and said, "I ain't got nothing to say."

"Fine, if that's the way you want to play it, let's go pay a visit to the sheriff," said Tucker. The others in the room watched with surprise as Art and Jake dragged Slim out of there while agent Tucker picked up the coins and followed them to the sheriff's office. They put him in the cell at the office and the sheriff got his name out of him. Agent Tucker, standing near the bars of the cell, said, "Okay, Slim who you been with and where'd the other man go?

"Why should I tell you anything unless there's something in it for me?" said Slim.

"Well, we have you with stolen gold coins so you're going to go down for having stolen property at the very least. Who knows how you got them…maybe we'll be slapping you with more charges."

"I didn't rob no one," Slim said, spitting on the floor of the cell.

"If you cooperate, I might be able to make it so you serve less time.

Slim looked interested. "Go on," he said.

"I want to know where you got them coins," Tucker said. "And I need to know who the man you were with is, and whereabouts he's headed."

What Tucker didn't know was that Slim was busy thinking hard about his predicament. He realized that if he told Tucker the truth, he would eventually be linked to the death of the three people. Since he didn't shoot anyone, he worried. How could he prove he wasn't one of those who did the shooting? In the end, he decided to tell them only part of what he knew.

"Okay first off, I only know him as Big John and I don't know for sure where he went. I think he went towards St. Louis. He said he was leaving and wasn't going to let me go with him because I let people see my gold coins, shortly before you showed up."

Slim looked up at Tucker and Tucker nodded. "Go on," he said.

"Well, we got the gold just outside Kansas City, Kansas where we pretended to be guides for a group of men and then stole their wagons. Big John and the others—besides me there was seven other people—they did some shoot'n while me and a couple others was take'n the wagons. I jumped on one of the wagons and drove on down the road. I don't know what happened to the men they were shooting at, I just hightailed it out of there. We got away with three wagons that had three strong boxes of gold in each wagon. We divided it up between the nine of us and split up."

Tucker glared at him, unsure if the man was being truthful.

Slim stood up and came to the bars. "I can take you to the place it happened, and I think I'll be able to recognize who it was we took it from, if we can find them around there."

Tucker saw something suspicious in the man's eyes, but he didn't know that Slim's idea was to escape as they ventured along the trail. A lot of things could happen traveling that far a distance.

"Where's the rest of the gold that you have?" Agent Tucker asked.

"Over at the livery stable in the stuff I was hauling on my pack mules, same as Big John's set up," he answered.

Tucker sent Jake and Art to check out the man's story. He asked the sheriff if he could put together a posse to go after Big John. The sheriff replied, "I'll be glad to ask around, but I don't think I can get any volunteers for something that didn't happen here. I'll go ask around and let you know in a few minutes, but don't get your hopes up."

In about thirty minutes, Art and Jake returned. Art

said, "We found his pack mules and his stuff at the livery, along with his share the gold. Let's get this locked up in the sheriff's safe."

Tucker nodded. At least he was telling some truth.

The sheriff returned and told Tucker that he couldn't get anyone willing to chase Big John. He also had with him a wire from the other agents that came in before agent Tucker arrived in Kingdom City. He said, "I'm sorry I didn't get you this wire sooner. The man in the telegraph office thought if it was urgent, I would've checked to see if something had come in for me and I'd have come to get it."

Tucker nodded his head and took the wire from the sheriff. He read it quietly to himself. The wire informed Agent Tucker what had happened in Columbia, where he'd sent Cody, Jared and Will. Since Agent Tucker wasn't sure where Big John was headed, he decided to wire St. Louis and tell the sheriff there they should be on the lookout for a man by himself with three mules coming into town. He was relieved that he now had the best lead they've had in a year on who might have actually taken the gold.

"Okay Slim, you earned yourself a trip back to where you came from. I need to find out who you took the gold from."

The next morning agent Tucker sent a wire back to Cody, Jared and Will in Columbia and told them to head to Kansas City, Kansas. He sent another wire to Clinton, telling Thaddeus, Dale and Jim where he was headed and to wait there in Clinton until he contacted them again with further instructions. After they picked up some supplies for the trip, Tucker, Jake and Art took one of the mules and they all left, heading towards Kansas City. The group consisted of three Rangers, a thief handcuffed and tied to the saddle of his horse and one unhappy mule.

Chapter 14

On to Deadwood

William, Roby and Tom, who were heading to Deadwood, were well on their way by the time the Pinkertons started out towards Kansas City, Kansas. Mountain Man Sam turned out to be for real and William could tell the man really knew what he was doing as far as guiding folks.

"It's gonna be relatively easy traveling until we get about halfway through the Nebraska territory," he said as they started out. "At that point, we're gonna have to be on the lookout for Indians."

He explained to William who rode next to him that there were two main Indian groups he worried about; the Kiowa and the Sioux.

"Since food is scarce in the wintertime the Indians sometimes want travelers to pay something to them for coming across their territory," Sam said. "Sometimes they come up and tell the travelers what they want, but other times they attack and take everything, depending on how desperate they are in their village for food."

William whistled quietly to himself.

"It also depends on how big of a group we are," Sam continued. "They don't like to attack a group unless they outnumber the group 2 to 1."

"We're a pretty small group," said Roby from behind. He and Tom had been listening.

"Yep. And small groups are the preferred prey." Sam said. "Iffen they attack, they usually leave no survivors."

The men all looked at each other but remained quiet.

"Not that I would know. It's gossip only," said Sam. "I've never been attacked."

The men chuckled at that, but William could tell by their faces they were tense. If it was just gossip, then they would be okay. And Sam said it had never happened to him. That was a good sign too.

At that moment Sam said, "Okay men, we're getting' close to Indian Territory and it won't be long before we start seeing a few Indians watching us from their horses in the distance."

Roby upon hearing this said, "Why didn't you tell us about this before we left?"

"I did," replied Sam. "I told you it was a dangerous trip, there were robbers and killers who wouldn't think twice about taking on a small group and I also told you that we had to go through Indian Territory."

"Yeah, but you didn't go into the details of why the Indians were gonna be a problem. Regular white men, robbers and such, we figured we could handle them, but starving Indians is a whole other situation. Are you tellin' us they pretty much feel they don't have a choice, like it's either take our stuff or starve to death over the winter?" Roby said,

"Let's just hope they'll be content with what we can give them, because they will eventually come up to us. Even if they have the idea of attacking us, they'll come up to size up what we have and how many of us they'll have to deal with. If it's just a small hunting party, they may be happy if we give them enough of our stuff. That's why I had you buy extra food and blankets so we could give it away and still have enough for ourselves. That just might be enough to get us through their territory, because when they get back to their village, they will tell everyone about us and at least that village won't attack us because they gave their word to let us pass through," Sam said.

A long silence followed. Then Sam said, "These Indians are proud people, and they believe in honoring their agreements. They'll make sure that any other encampments or villages of their tribe will know to leave us alone if we've already paid what was asked. If you turn around and decide to go back after going through the territory, you'll probably have to pay again, or if we end up crossing another tribe's territory, same thing."

After hearing that, the McCoys decided they had best keep a close eye out all around, because who knew when they would be crossing into a tribe's territory?

William and Tom would be watching the right and left, Roby would keep an eye out behind them, and Sam would be keeping his attention on the trail ahead.

They weren't making very good time because of the deep snow on the trail. No travelers had been on it, so they were blazing the trail through the snow for the next people or at least until the next snowstorm. After two days of barely 10 miles each day, Sam told them he thought it was time to abandon the wagons and load the stuff on the mules.

Tom asked, "Can we just try one more day and see if it gets any better? If it doesn't then I guess that's what we have to do."

Sam agreed, adding that he didn't think it would get better. "It's winter out here men, and these parts get a lot of snow."

William started wondering how they were going to load the gold without Sam seeing it or being curious as to what was so heavy. On the next day Sam spotted three Indians on a ridge a good ways away watching them and following along. After an hour or so there were only two Indians following them.

"Listen up men," he said. "I want you to keep your heads down and listen to me. Do not look up. There are Indians on the ridge. When you get a chance and it don't seem too obvious, take a look."

One by one, they glanced toward the ridge. Then, Sam noticed there were no longer three Indians.

"Get ready. We're probably going to get a visit, depending how far away the village is. They've sent one brave back to get some more men. Hopefully, they're going to just do that, to give us a show of force and not to gather a war party."

They kept traveling at the same pace trying not to show any fear or alert the Indians that they knew about them. Sam told them that most of the time these Indians wouldn't attack at night, at least they were not known for that.

"They are fighters, but they normally fight fair," he said.

The men decided to camp that night right on the trail and everyone slept near his wagon. At sunrise, 12 Indian braves rode up on the wagons, six on each side. Their leader walked his horse forward and Sam walked up to him. These were Sioux Indians and Sam had dealt with this particular tribe before. Knowing this was a good source for supplies for his village because of the previous times he had dealt with Sam, he was friendly. William watched the exchange with interest, his respect for Mountain Man Sam growing by the minute. It seemed to him that the two men, Sam and the Chief, were almost like friends. Sam apparently knew the Sioux language, at least enough to bargain with him. William realized that Sam was full of surprises. He looked at his kin, Roby and Tom, and they each seemed to be thinking the same thing.

When he was finished talking, Sam turned to the McCoys and said, "Okay you remember the extra foodstuffs I told you to bring, get out the extra barrels of flour, beans, and fatback. They should be on the backs of your wagons, just pull the tarps back far enough so you can get to that stuff, so you won't have to expose anything else to their view. Also grab the stack of extra blankets. Then put everything together on the road behind us, so it will look like a big pile of supplies and they will be happy with it and will be satisfied with what they're going to take back to the village."

The McCoys did as they were told. The air was frigid, and their breath was steamy. A cold wind howled through the Plains and moving the supplies was work on their cold hands. When they were finished, they went back to their wagons.

Sam made a big show about how much stuff he was giving them, and the Indian seemed proud and happy for what he was going to bring back to the village. Apparently, the Indian told him to go in peace and they would meet again in peace.

Sam then said to the McCoys, "Everyone climb on the wagons and move out slowly just like we had been traveling while they were watching us, and everything will be fine."

That's exactly what happened. The Indians let them go and were content with the bounty they had received. When they traveled a little ways further, the McCoys finally relaxed a little bit and were breathing easier. They talked about how it had seemed to them like a close call.

"I'm surprised they didn't want our mules," William said.

"It wasn't really a close call," Sam said. "I know that Indian and he knows he can count on me for supplies several times a year, so he wasn't about to ruin a good thing by taking our means of hauling our stuff or killing us. Plus, he knows what traveling is going to be like this time a year and if he made it so we couldn't get through, I might have a hard time getting more people to guide through here and that would put an end to his getting more supplies."

They traveled till the end of the day and the snow was deepening at the same time the terrain was growing steeper. They decided they would abandon the wagons the next day, and since they didn't have as much cargo, it might possibly fit on their mules.

So, the next morning they began to pack their things on the mules. Just when they were ready to load the gold, William, as they had planned, asked Sam to help him get some fresh meat. He agreed to give it a try for a short while but if they didn't find anything, Sam knew about a valley further on where game was plentiful at this time a year.

While Sam and William were gone hunting, Roby and Tom quickly loaded the gold onto their mules. When they'd finished, only a few items were left behind, all things they could do without. After about an hour and a half, William and Sam came back empty handed, but ready to get back on the trail. They tied all their mules together in a string and put the lead rope around their saddles. They made better time like this, traveling almost eighteen miles the first day compared to the ten miles a day that they had been getting. Satisfied with the distance they had gone that day, they made camp early and gave their mules some extra grain for their work. Three more days passed, and they saw more Indians watching them—fifteen on horseback.

"I thought we paid them off. Are we going to have to pay again?" William asked.

"Hard to say. We may have come into another tribe's territory. Those Indians don't look the same. They look like another tribe that I'm not familiar with. We need to keep our eyes peeled because this might just get dangerous here."

A few hours went by and four of the Indians stopped their horses across the trail in front of them. Sam rode out to try and communicate. Although he tried speaking, the language was different, and he didn't understand much and wasn't sure if they understood him. Through gestures he was able to say he could give them some provisions, but they didn't have much to give. He came back to the wagons and asked everyone to put some things in a blanket from each of their provisions. What they were able to give seemed very small in comparison to what they had given the other Indians. The four Indians took what was offered and rode off. They left a strange feeling in the air, and William felt nervous.

Sam told them, "I think these are Kiowa Indians and I don't think they're very happy with what we had to give. We'll need to post guards tonight, and every night from here on in."

"I noticed only two of them had rifles," Roby said.

"Yes," said Sam. "One was a military single shot and the other was one of the new Sharps repeaters. I didn't see any belts with bullets, but they could've been carrying extra ammunition in the pouches I saw hanging off the sides of the horses. You'll need to prepare the Sharps you have and have extra ammunition on you at all times. When we stop for the night, we need to stop in an area where there is some dry wood that we can use to keep a fire going all night. I have no idea whether these Indians will attack at night or not."

When they stopped for the night, they all got busy preparing their weapons and ammunition, keeping one rifle with them and their pockets full of bullets. They each placed an extra rifle against the mule packs and ammunition next to it.

The night passed without incident, but at sunrise Sam noticed movement in the brush and yelled out a warning, "Here they come, grab your rifles and find some cover."

Immediately after he said that the silence of the morning erupted into war cries and whoops from the Indians charging the campsite. The first shots that came from the Indians didn't hit anyone and William, Roby and Tom returned fire killing at least three. But in moments, they realized, they were completely surrounded by about 30 Indians. There were only a few rifle shots coming from the Indians, but lots of arrows were flying. The night before they had piled their supplies in a circle leaving one mule with one box of gold and one mule with some supplies loaded on their backs for each of them, just in case. If they had to make a quick escape, they wouldn't lose everything. After the initial charge, the Indians dropped back and Sam and the McCoys were able to get inside the circle of supplies, using it for cover. The Indians had regrouped and formed a plan on how to attack again. They charged from all sides, arrows and bullets flying at them from both sides of their barricade of supplies. Sam took an arrow in the shoulder during the melee and Tom took a bullet in the side. William pulled the arrow from Sam's shoulder and Roby checked out Tom's wound and tried as best he could to stop the bleeding.

The Indians saw that they had wounded two of them, even though they lost a few more of their own. The loss though, seemed to only make them more determined to take what they came for. They charged again, but the McCoys, even though wounded, were prepared and started shooting before the Indians could get close enough to be accurate with their arrows. The McCoys hit three or four more which meant the Indians were down in numbers not to their liking—William figured that meant about half of their braves were still healthy, a few were wounded and seven were dead. They backed off out of range of the rifles and seemed content to wait it out. Every once in a while, a rifle shot came from the Indians, usually hitting the supply packs but always coming from a different direction. This went on until almost dusk.

"We need to make a break for it when it gets dark." Sam said. "They know we're trapped, and they can take all the time they need."

The Indians made one more heavy charge just before

dark and when they retreated Sam and William looked around and realized that Roby had taken an arrow in the leg and that Tom had been shot in the head during the last attack. William ran over to his kin and knelt beside him. He knew Tom was dead. William and Roby, who lay injured, exchanged glances but said nothing.

They were down to three men now and only one, William, was healthy. The moon had come up. Although not bright, they could see about 50 feet around them fairly well because of the white backdrop of the snow, so the Indians were not going to be able to sneak up very close. They could make out their horses and mules who were very agitated and moving back and forth and side to side as much as the ropes would let them. William managed to sneak over to where the horses and mules were all tied together so they couldn't run off, and he got the saddles on three of the horses. He then made his way back to the others.

"You're going to have to help each other get to the horses, while I try to cover you as you make your way there," said William to Sam and Roby. William realized he had a tremendous responsibility now that he was the only healthy one of the three. He was nervous.

"I'll do the best I can while I'm trying to get the six mules we have ready to leave, untied and over to the horses," he said. "I'm going to cut the other animals lose. I think it's our only chance to give them something else to think about, other than us."

They looked at him seeming not to understand what he had in mind. "I'm hoping they're more interested in seeing what we got in our mule packs and rounding up the animals then in chasing us for the moment, and it might just give us a chance to get away," William said.

Putting as many bullets in their pockets as possible and filling a couple of cloth bags with more, they were ready to make their break for it. Coming out from behind their cover, shots rang out from the Indians and arrows started hitting around them. With Sam, who was injured the least between the two injured, trying to help Roby get to the horses they were a big, slow moving target. William fired back in the direction of the rifle shots, not being able to tell if he hit anything. He just hoped he could keep them from shooting accurately while he attempted to get over to the mules. He made it to the mules, freed all of those that were unloaded and the extra horses. He saw several of the Indians give chase after the animals.

Next, William disconnected the mules that were loaded and pulled them over to the horses. While he was tying the ropes around the saddle horns, Sam was trying to help Roby get on a horse. That's when Roby was hit in the back by two arrows just as he almost got in the saddle. He fell back to the ground, mortally wounded. Seeing that, Sam tried to get on the horse closest to him. He managed to get a foot in the stirrup and hook his arm around the pommel of the saddle, keeping himself shielded on at least one side by the body of the horse.

William had tied one set of mules to each of the other saddles. He went over to Roby to see how he was and could tell he was already dead. He quickly climbed on the horse that was closest, checking the wrapping of the rope around the saddle horn. He let out a yell, "Hee Yaa," and slapped Sam's horse on the rear while kicking his heels into the sides of the horse he was on. Both horses bolted forward and ran off into the night as fast as they could go pulling the mules with them. The mules quickly gained the pace of the frightened horses sprinting away into the darkness. With the moon rising the dark night had brightened. Thankfully the snow on the ground made it easy for them to see the trail they had been following.

The horses didn't need to be guided and they ran for all they were worth back the way they had come the day before. Once past the last of the Indians, Sam managed pull himself upright in the saddle and hang on. After about 20 minutes, they had to slow the horses down for fear of killing them. They stopped for a second to listen for any pursuers but heard nothing. They continued at a slow trot, trying to let their horses catch their breath. After about ten more minutes, Sam said, "We need to walk them, or they won't last through the night and we need to keep moving all night."

William was right in thinking the Indians would put more value on the animals and supplies than on them. Though he hadn't seen it, he was sure the Indians had taken the time to recover all the mules and horses and gather the mule packs to see what was inside. William imagined that when they found all kinds of things they could use, like guns and ammunition, foodstuffs and heavy boxes of gold coins (which they probably knew must be something of great value), that they would feel victorious. Surely by then, they'd figured out how the mule packs were fastened to the mules and loaded them up with all the bounty they had taken from the men. William could see it in his mind: how they then set out for their village, beaming with pride and the thoughts of how they would be heroes to the village when they returned. He shook his head, as if to empty it of thoughts. His losses had been great.

William and Sam made it back to the Sioux Indian territory and were quickly approached by the same Indians they had met on the way in. Sam explained to their leader what had happened, and the chief noticed that Sam was injured in his shoulder and insisted that they come to his village, where he had the Indian squaws tend to his wound. Two days later they left the village heading back to Kansas City.

"I feel awful bad about what happened," said Sam. "The least I can do is offer you your money back."

William responded saying, "No, that's not right, we knew the risks and we were all willing to pay up front so that in case something did happen, you would have been paid. You keep the money, you earned it, even though it turned out bad. Heck, you almost lost your own skin, so don't fret over it. You did what you promised, what happened was not your fault. Let's just get back to my kinfolk in Kansas City."

CHAPTER 15

THE BRAXTON SISTERS

The day after William, Roby and Tom left with Sam, Willy and Festus went into town to buy some supplies. They were wrapping the reins of their horses around the hitching post in front of the general store, when two young ladies in their early twenties came out the front door of the store. They were dressed in jeans and flannel shirts with cowboy boots on their feet, looking like ranch hands, but very pretty ranch hands. Willy and Festus quickly glanced at each other. All it took was for their eyes to meet and it was a race up the steps to the ladies. The ladies were startled by the quickness of the men coming up the steps.

Willy acted as if he hadn't seen them when he got to the top of the steps and stopped abruptly saying, "I'm sorry, I didn't mean to startle you ladies."

"That's okay, no harm done, just surprised by your quickness," said the closest one to him.

When Willy stopped so quickly, Festus almost ran into the back of him and had to put his hands out to stop himself. Looking up at the ladies he smiled and said, "Whoa, sorry about this, but sure is nice to have almost run into a couple of pretty ladies like yourselves."

The two women looked at each other, eyes wide and smiling. Willy took stock of the way the ladies looked and him and Festus. They seemed to approve of their looks. The one that looked like she might be a year or so older than the other said, "Just glad you looked up soon enough to stop in time, so we didn't have to defend ourselves and hurt you."

They looked at each other and grinned. These were two beautiful women who also could handle themselves if the need arose, thought Willy. Impressed by their beauty and their inner strength, the two McCoys were mesmerized.

Willy said, "That's all I'd need is to have stories going around town about how I got whupped by a woman."

The younger one added, "Don't worry we wouldn't hurt you that bad, just enough to learn your lesson."

Festus spoke up, "Well, seeing that we made fools of ourselves, can we at least help you with your supplies or offer you lunch in the café?"

Willy quickly interjected, "Where's your manners Festus they don't even know our names and we haven't even been introduced. I'm Willy McCoy and this here's Festus McCoy and might we have the pleasure of learning your names?"

The two women looked at each other slightly blushing and smiling. It was clear they were both interested in the two men standing in front of them.

The older of the two said, "I'm Clara and this is my sister, Sarah Bell."

Clara was the taller of the two, very elegant and regal looking. She had high cheekbones, and a gorgeous smile. Her skin was fair and unblemished, and her dark curls fell around her shoulders. She seemed more confident than her sister, and maybe slightly more intelligent. But what Sarah might have lacked in elegance and smarts, she made up for in personality. Charming, funny and cute, with a bright smile, and lovely skin, freckled across the bridge of her nose, her eyes had a sparkle to them. Long hair, a shade lighter than her sister's, with golden highlights, snaked down her back in a long braid. She had delicate hands and held a comely leather clutch between her fingers. Both women seemed strong and capable, but definitely feminine.

"We're right pleased and proud to meet you," said Willy. "Now what do you think of our offer to help or buy you lunch?" Willy said.

"We still got a few places to stop and Mr. Hastings, the store owner, will load our wagon which we already have around back. But by the time we're through with our additional errands, it should be lunchtime."

Willy and Festus both smiled in a relaxed way. It was clear to Willy that the ladies seemed taken with them both.

Clara said, "We could meet you at the Bluebonnet Café down the street. I do believe you boys have some chores to get done in town yourselves, so that ought to work out good for both of us."

Hearing that, Willy's smile went from ear to ear. "That would be perfect, if we get done first, we'll wait for you out in front of the café," he said.

As soon as the words were out of his mouth, he took his hat off and Festus did the same, following Willy's lead, and said, "It's been a pleasure to meet you ladies and we hope to see you later."

With their hats in their hands in front of them they nodded their heads in respect and stepped aside to let the ladies pass. The ladies nodded in return.

"Until later then, see you boys at the café," said Sarah. As they walked down the steps to the street, Festus and Willy saw the ladies' heads leaning towards each other as if they were discussing something secret. Not too familiar with the ways of women, Willy wondered what they were saying. Festus and Willy exchanged glances.

"Do you think they'll really come?" Festus asked.

Willy shrugged. But he said, "Yep, I sure do."

The two men went into the general store and up to the counter where a man stood. He'd been watching the scene on his porch between the women and men. He knew the McCoys from other times they had been in and knew they were honest and sincere when they spoke.

"I see you've met the Braxton sisters," he said to Willy and Festus. "Mind you best be on your good behavior around them. They won't take to any disrespect towards anyone and especially anyone that underestimates what they are capable of."

"They sure are strong women," said Festus. "And pretty, too."

The shopkeeper said, "I've watched them grow up and take over their ranch when their parents passed away and they have run it as well as any man and probably better. They're right proper ladies and deserve to be treated as such."

"So, their last name is Braxton?" Festus asked. "Is that name supposed to mean something around here?"

"You bet it does," said Mr. Hastings. "They've been here since the town was founded and their father was once mayor. His ranch got so big he had to stay on it as much as possible making sure his ranch hands were doing all the work that was needed in the way he wanted it done. Due to that, he gave up being mayor."

"What about their mother," he asked.

Mr. Hastings looked at the ground then said, "They lost their mother when they were about 12-years-old, but he taught his daughters how to run the ranch like he ran it. I think maybe they've done a better job than he did. Been do'n it since he went off to fight the war and never came back."

Festus and Willy nodded their heads. Willy thought that he liked a woman who could be that pretty and still manage a ranch better than a man. That was someone, he thought, that he'd like to try and keep up with.

"So," said Mr. Hastings, "What can I do for you boys today?"

Festus piped up. "We need some pitch and some nails and a roll of binding wire cuz we got some fences and some buckets to fix."

"You'll find all of that along the far wall in different sizes. Since you know how much you're going to need you can go help yourself to what you're looking for. I'll be in the back loading the Braxton's wagon. Just give me a shout when you're ready," said Mr. Hastings.

They didn't need much and what they got would fit in the satchel that they brought with them, which they could wrap around the saddle horn. They called Mr. Hastings when they were ready, paid for their supplies and went outside to the horses. As they rode down the street, they looked on both sides for the two ladies, but didn't see them. They decided to pass the time waiting in front of the Bluebonnet Café. They tied the horses to the hitching post and waited in the cold, watching the leaves fall from the trees.

It wasn't long before they saw the two ladies walking on the boardwalk towards the café. As they arrived, the two McCoys stood up and took off their hats smiling.

"Pretty good timing, we've only been here a couple of minutes," said Willy.

"We finished our errands quickly today," said Clara.

The four of them entered and were told to sit wherever they liked. After holding the chairs for the ladies, the McCoys sat down.

"When we come here, we usually just get the daily special," Sarah said. "But everything's pretty good."

They all ordered the day's special. They made small

talk about the weather, and the McCoys told them about the ranch they had rented for the winter. Clara spoke up, "Have you heard about the Thanksgiving Day dance coming up?"

Neither of the McCoys had been in town much lately, so they hadn't seen or heard anything about it. Both men shook their heads and said no at the same time. This made the ladies giggle. Festus looked at Sarah and liked the way she blushed just a little bit when she laughed.

"Well," Clara said, her brown eyes twinkling in the direction of Willy, "Every year we have the Thanksgiving dance at the town hall. The festivities start about two in the afternoon. It's a real fun time."

"There's lots of food and things to do, with a dance following in the evening," Sarah said. Her cheeks were pink, and she seemed excited about the dance.

"Do you think it would be too forward of us to ask you if we may escort you to the Thanksgiving Day Dance?" Festus asked.

Willy shot him a quick glance. Festus looked embarrassed.

"Slow down Mr. Racehorse," said Sarah. "We just met you and I think you're both nice gentleman and seem to have good intentions, but we still don't know enough about you."

"However," Clara interrupted, "if we were to meet you there, that wouldn't really count as courting, now, would it?"

Sarah nodded. "I think that Clara may be right. And I can speak for the both of us when I say that we'd be willing to meet you there and enjoy the festival together,"

"Okay then," said Festus, "We will see you at the Thanksgiving Day Festival."

The four of them enjoyed the rest of their meal and when it was over, Willy paid the bill. After that they walked out together and stopped to watch the afternoon foot traffic on the street. Horses carrying men with their purchases and women together or with children walked by in the cold, coats pulled tight, and hats drawn down.

"Much obliged for the lunch, Gentlemen," Clara said. "It was nice meeting you both,"

The two McCoys put on their hats but bowed their heads signaling their pleasure.

"Well, then," said Clara. "We have much to do back home before nightfall. We thank you kindly for the company."

"You're welcome," said Festus, looking briefly into Sarah's eyes. Her face bloomed with a blush. Willy and Clara exchanged glances of a more mature nature and then the ladies walked down the steps and into the street, disappearing quickly into a notions shop next door.

Willy and Festus couldn't help but look at each other and grin from ear to ear,

"We sure were lucky coming into town today and being at the store right when they came out," said Festus.

"Yeah, couldn't have been any better iffen we had planned it," replied Willy.

"They sure are pretty," Festus said.

Willy jokingly tipped the hat off Festus's head, but Festus, being quick, caught it.

"You couldn't be more obvious if I paid you to try," said Willy.

"What?" he said innocently.

The men laughed, having fully enjoyed their afternoon, and their friendship with each other. They went for their horses, and headed back to the ranch, their purchases ready for the afternoon of chores left to do.

• • •

During the next ten days before Thanksgiving, the two McCoys bragged to their kinfolk about the ladies they met and how they were going to meet them at the dance. They even went to town three times hoping to "bump into them" again. They didn't find them any of the times they went. Festus wanted to go out to their ranch and pay them a visit, but Willy, who had more experience with women than Festus did, told him unless they were invited that wouldn't be a good idea.

"You're right, of course," Festus said, "but I sure would like to see that pretty Sarah."

"I can only say I'm glad she's the one you fancy."

"Clara is more your type anyways," said Festus.

"And what type is that?"

"Oh, you know, intelligent and in control."

Willy shrugged. "She's pretty, too."

Festus said, "Sarah's the pretty one."

Willy didn't take the bait. He only hoped that Sarah favored Festus and Clara preferred him.

CHAPTER 16

THANKSGIVING DAY

The day of the dance they dressed in their best clothes, boots and hats. They were so anxious they went into town at noon even though the festivities wouldn't be starting till two in the afternoon. They left their horses in a livery for the day and went down to the town hall. Both men were amazed to see how busy everyone was at putting the festival together. People were preparing tables and food. Shopkeepers and craftsmen were setting their wares—leather goods, marmalade and jellies, plus canned fruit and wine—on shelves in recently constructed booths. There was a stall with popcorn balls and one with freshly made candied apples. Confectioners and whisky makers too. Free lemonade and water was available for the volunteers setting things up as well as for the townspeople that came to take part in the festival.

There were notices on boards announcing games and events scheduled for later on. As more people began to trickle in, an announcer promoted some of the games: The turkey shoot, and a foot race. Big Windy's were announced, where people would compete in telling the best, and wildest stories imaginable.

As far as Willy could tell, the turkey shoot was the most popular event. The winner would receive a turkey raised by a family named Neffle. They had a reputation for raising the biggest and tastiest turkeys in town.

"Let's enter this thing," said Festus.

"Okay," Willy agreed.

After they entered, Willy kept watching the road for the ladies to arrive. He noticed Festus trying to act casual as he scaled the crowds of people that were arriving.

"Listen," said Willy. "We'll find those ladies when we find 'em. Let's you and me go watch them set up that turkey shoot."

Just then, Willy felt someone tapping his shoulder. Festus must have felt something too, because they both turned around at the same time. There behind them were the two most stunning ladies they had ever seen, each wearing beautiful fall dresses. Clara wore a sensible off-white gown, not too flashy, with red roses sewn along the hem and her sister wore black, with silk buttons all the way down the back. They looked fresh-faced and, as far as the men were concerned, they were the two most beautiful women at the festival. Willy was also glad to see that Clara had tapped his shoulder and Sarah had tapped Festus's which told him that the two women had made a decision about which of them they preferred. It lined up with their preferences and a moment passed when Festus and Willy winked at each other. Festus looked at Sarah, her cheeks pink and her smile wide and nodded his head. He had also hoped she would be the one for him. Willy was equally glad to see that Clara had chosen him.

"We were hoping you were still coming, and nothing had come up that would cause you to miss the dance," Willy said.

"Nothing would make us miss this dance," said Clara smiling radiantly.

Festus asked if they would like some lemonade and offered that he would fetch it. Coming back with the lemonades, Festus suggested that they walk around for a few minutes before the turkey shoot started. They confessed they had entered the contest.

"We've been around so long we have an automatic entry," Sarah told them.

"Oh, so we're going up against you?" Asked Willy.

"Well, the contest is open to everyone, so it won't be just us," Sarah replied. "But I have to warn you, Clara won it last year."

Clara looked at Willy and she humbly said, "I was just lucky."

Somehow, he didn't believe it was just a matter of luck, and he realized neither did she.

Nearby, children were bobbing for apples, a three-legged race, limited to couples, was about to start, and up next was a gunnysack race.

They walked over to watch the races. They heard an announcement about the pie-eating contest which would take place right after the turkey shoot.

"I wonder what kind of pie it will be," Festus said.

"It'll definitely be something that will smear all over your face, probably either berry cobbler or chocolate pudding pie," said Sarah.

It was then they heard the announcement that the turkey shoot was about to start. They joined the other contestants where the contest was set up. One of the judges, a man dressed up in a top hat and wearing a suit, explained the rules.

"There will be two phases of shooting, and a winner will be chosen from each one. One phase is pistols and the other, rifles."

They were told that they could use their own weapons or use the weapons they had provided for the shoot. These included two of the new Sharps rifles and colt revolvers. There were 27 contestants battling for the targets and the chance to win a turkey.

For the pistol shooting they had two standing targets, one at 20 yards and one at 40 yards with bull's-eyes. They would also throw a tin can in the air to be shot at. The second portion was the rifle shooting. In that one of the targets started at 50 yards, then one at 100 yards and one at 150 yards. The contestants would get three shots at each target and their totals would determine the winner.

The contestants all took their turns with the pistols and when they totaled up the points there were six people tied. These included two ranchers that Festus and Willy had never met, and Sarah and Clara, and Festus and Willy. The judges were amazed and announced that this was the first time in the history of their Thanksgiving Festival that they had more than two people tied in points.

They put a pistol target at 60 yards and threw two cans in the air at the same time for the pistol part of the competition. The two ranchers missed two of their shots at the 60-yard targets and only hit one of the cans. The ladies each hit two of their shots at the 60-yard targets and both of the cans that were tossed in the air. The McCoys were not sure what they should do. They huddled as they watched the ladies make their shots.

"They're darned good," whispered Festus.

"I had a feeling," said Willy. "I know we can probably beat them."

"I wouldn't be so sure," said Festus.

"Well, either way, don't you kinda want them to win?"

"I was going to say the same thing," said Festus.

"Let's try for a tie," said Willy.

Just then their names were called. Both Clara and Sarah had caught them whispering, and Willy saw them giggling, but also looking just a bit satisfied. When Willy and Clara met eyes, Clara raised one eyebrow and Willy broke out into a grin.

The cans were tossed in the air, both men took aim and, surprising everyone, both men hit both cans.

The judge said, "Let's throw three cans at the same time."

People watching the competition clapped and hooted. They had drawn a crowd

"In case these boys are holding back we're going to make them shoot first at the three cans," said one of the judges.

More hoots and whistles. People were having a good time watching this competition between the McCoy boys and the Braxton girls. Willy noticed most everyone seemed to be rooting for Clara and Sarah.

The cans were tossed in the air and both McCoys missed one each. Afterward they looked at each other and nodded so only they could see.

When it was the ladies' turn to shoot, they both strolled up looking calm and composed. They both were smiling, and Sarah went first. When the cans flew through the air, Sarah fired away, missing one herself. Clara was next. The more composed of the two, the judges knew what a good shot she was. To Willy, who watched intently, the judges threw the cans up and she made her shots perfectly, hitting all three.

The crowd went wild. Willy was happy to see how much these ladies were liked in town.

"Congratulations little miss sure shot," announced the judge, "Our winner for the pistols, for the second year in a row is Clara Braxton. Now onto the rifle portion."

Once again, the competition came down to the same six people. The two ranchers hit the can one time each and did not hit the pumpkin. The ladies hit the can all three times and hit the pumpkins that were placed after each of them had shot twice. The third pumpkin remained untouched for both ladies after their third shot. The McCoys, taking their time, made each shot count and hit each target. So now it was down to determining which McCoy was going to take home the turkey. The contest workers put a smaller target; a vegetable can at 100 yards and a medium- sized pumpkin at 150 yards for each of them in the rifle portion. Willy and Festus took turns, and each hit the smaller tin can and the pumpkin.

"Well folks," said the judge. "We can't be out here all afternoon shoot'n, so if we don't get a winner after this next target, you're both going to get turkeys."

The folks watching seemed to take a liking to the McCoys, and many clapped and laughed.

"I'm going to have someone throw the can at 100 yards out," said the judge. "This is the most difficult shot we've ever tried in our competition since it began. Let's see if it can be done."

He signaled the thrower of the can to give it a toss. The can could barely be seen going through the air. Willy was at the ready when it went in the air and he quickly got a bead and fired. The can jumped in the air, signaling a hit and then applause roared from the crowd.

Festus looked at him and said, "Show off. I don't think I've ever tried to make a shot like this, so I don't stand a chance since I know you used to shoot birds out of the air at this distance."

People in the crowd hearing him, laughed. Willy just smiled, content with his success. The can flew up and Festus tried his best. After his first shot missed, he fired quickly once more and you could see the can bounce in the air, so he'd actually hit the can, but not on the first shot.

The crowd once again hooted and clapped.

The judge shouted over the crowd, "Okay folks, I say that that second shot don't count so I'm callin' this contest for both Willy and Clara."

The applause was loud as the crowd had grown in size. Willy and Clara were given blue ribbons and handed a turkey while everyone applauded their marksmanship. The judge told them they would keep the turkeys in a cool place for them to pick up when they were ready to leave.

"You're a good shot," Willy said.

Clara, smiling at Willy, said, "You're not so bad a shot yourself. Where'd you learn to shoot like that?"

Responding truthfully, Willy said, "Growing up we didn't have much money to buy lead for bullets, so we learned to make each shot count." He thought a second and then added, "Course nowadays we have those factory-made bullets and back then we had lead balls that we made ourselves and black powder which was not as accurate."

They walked together in silence for a minute. Willy liked the way she listened to him.

After a moment he said, "Why don't we go over and see what kind of pie they have at that contest. I'm a little hungry."

Festus added he might give it a try also.

Willy offered Clara his elbow, and Festus, watching

Willy did the same for Sarah. Together, the two couples walked towards the pie-eating contest. When they arrived at the tables where the contest was going to be held, Willy realized the contestants were going to have to keep their hands behind their back while they tried to eat the pies.

Looking slightly embarrassed at the ladies he said, "I might be a little hungry, but I don't want to be getting my face covered with sticky pie filling and probably get it all over my clothes too. I think I'll pass on this contest."

Festus had said he'd give it a try but then, after what Willy said, he quickly changed his mind. "You're probably right, not the best idea" he said.

Instead, the four of them watched as ten brave souls tried to eat as much pie as they could with their hands tied behind their backs, in the time allowed. There were some that stuck their entire face into the pie and had it all over their eyebrows and in their nose, with pieces sticking all over their cheeks. Others were trying to eat without getting it on their faces, but it was next to impossible to eat quickly and not get it all over them. It was quite amusing to watch and the four of them were laughing at the chaos and the good cheer.

It was announced that the apple race was about to start, and each team had to have four people so they thought they would join since they could all do it together. The winners received a bushel of apples to take home. The object was to pass apples between them and eventually to the fourth person who was then supposed to get it to a basket and drop it in. The trick was they couldn't use their hands or touch the apples with their hands. If that apple was dropped on the ground, you had to start over. The first person would get the apple placed under their chin and have to hold it there while trying to pass it to the next person, and at the end of the time allotted the team that had the most apples in their basket were the winners.

Festus was at the beginning and Willy was at the end, with the two ladies in the middle. It was quite comical to watch the men trying to get the apples from the ladies without allowing their bodies to touch each other. Though both of the McCoys were embarrassed, they knew they had no choice but to touch the women because of how close they would be.

Festus and Willie each dropped a couple of apples while passing or receiving the apples from the ladies because of their nerves. But Willy noticed that, again, both Clara and Sarah seemed calm and composed, laughing and enjoying themselves. At the end of the race, they had three apples in their basket and big smiles on their faces. As it turned out, some youngsters about 12-years-old won the bushel of apples.

They were all smiling, and Willy could see that everyone was having a grand time. Willy said, "You know this has been the most fun I've had in a long time."

Clara put her arm through his. "I'm glad to hear you say that."

Festus and Sarah walked ahead, and Willy watched

the two of them talking and laughing with each other.

"The dance is coming up," Clara said. She looked at the sky. "Sun's about to set."

They were near the dance hall and when the doors were opened, Clara suggested they go right away to find a table.

"I'm starting to get a little chilly anyway," she said. "It will be warm in there."

Sarah and Festus had already gone inside and found a table close to the dance floor. The two men held their chairs while the women took their seat, and Willy offered to get some apple cider. When the ladies said they'd like that, Willy told Festus to come give him a hand, and he dutifully followed over to the drink table. On their way over they noticed a lot of the young men in the dance hall eyeing them enviously, which made them quite proud that they were the ones the ladies had chosen for the dance.

Willy and Festus didn't say much to each other as they got the cider, but Willy could tell that Festus was enjoying himself as much as he was.

After bringing the drinks back to the table, Willy and Festus sat down. The music started. Willy was not shy, and he quickly stood up, and reached out for Clara's hand. Festus turned red, but Willy said, "C'mon, let's all dance." He watched Festus invite Sarah to dance, and they went to the dance floor. Neither of the McCoys danced much but Willy seemed to know what to do. Festus was slightly awkward, but Willy noticed the gentle way Sarah guided him, showing him steps and laughing sweetly for the fun. They were soon enjoying themselves and before long, Willy noticed, Festus was keeping pace quite well with his girl.

When they returned to their table for refreshments, some of the single men approached the sisters for a dance, but Willy was happy to see they both gracefully rejected the offers. At the end of the evening, they all felt very good about having passed the festival together. When it got late, the men offered to walk Clara and Sarah to their buggy. Before they did that, they picked up their turkeys.

At the buggy, Willy helped Clara in, and she surprised him by giving him a chaste kiss on the cheek. Before they rode off, Clara said, "We have a nice place for a picnic down by the stream that runs through our property. You can come by whenever you'd like for a lunch."

Sarah said, "We can't promise you we'll be able to join you should you come, at least not right away, because we have a lot of work every day to do on the ranch."

"But do come by and pay us a visit when you have the time and we'll see if we can't get away for an afternoon," Clara said. "Maybe we can cook up this turkey and make a meal and then some, out of them.

Festus responded, "We'll do just that. We'll be looking forward to it."

As the buggy turned, Clara said, "Thanks for the wonderful evening, we'll be looking forward to your visit, just follow the road out of town about two miles and you'll see our sign showing the direction to Braxton ranch, it'll be at the end of the road."

The two McCoys watched the ladies as they drove away in their buggy.

Festus turned to Willy, "She gave me a kiss on the cheek."

Willy grinned. "I got one, too."

Both men smiled all the way back to the ranch. When they rejoined their kin, they couldn't keep it to themselves; they had to tell all the others about everything they did and boastfully showing them the turkey and telling about how lovely, polite and exciting the ladies were. It was clear both were smitten over the two women, and some of the others teased them to no end. But some of the boys looked a little envious.

Willy and Festus both joked about they could hardly wait for a warm day. Then after two days of cold rain, the sun rose, and the earth warmed. Neither Festus, nor Willy could hold back their excitement and anticipation to see their ladies again. Once they were through with the chores for the day, they saddled up and took a leisurely ride out to the sisters' ranch.

CHAPTER 17

A PICNIC

Arriving there around 10:30 in the morning, they found Sarah in the corral looking over one of their horses. Clara was inside in the house. Sarah looked over at the two riders and was pleasantly surprised when she realized who they were. As luck would have it, they didn't have much planned in the way of work for themselves that day and had already given the ranch hands the jobs that were left.

"Well, hello there. Didn't think we would see you so soon," Sarah said.

"Well, as you requested, we waited for the warm day and here it was. So here we are," said Festus.

"I hope we didn't catch you on a day you have a lot of things to do," Willy said.

"I think today is a good day, let me check with Clara."

At that moment Clara stepped out onto the porch, curious to see who had come to the ranch. When she realized that it was Willy and Festus she smiled. She looked surprised but happy about it. "Hello boys. Looks like you missed us," she said.

Willy said, "Yes ma'am we did."

"And it's a perfectly nice day so we took advantage of it when we saw it," said Festus.

"We're very glad you did," said Clara. Sarah nodded her head in agreement.

Festus walked his horse over to Sarah and took his hat off when he reached her. "We were afraid you might forget about us if we waited too long," he said smiling.

"Don't count yourselves so short. That was the most fun we've had in a while," she replied.

Clara looked at Willy. "Shall we have a look around," she said. "This was my daddy's ranch. I'll show you around."

They walked over to the corral and Clara said, "I'm surprised you came so soon."

"Is that a bad thing?" he asked. "That we did."

"No," she said. "Not at all."

Willy liked the way the ladies looked. They were dressed in pants, but he knew that there were women who worked on ranches and even in the gold mines, who needed to wear pants out of necessity. He thought she looked fetching.

Clara showed Willy around. There was a small pond on the property, and they walked around it. Then they rejoined Clara and Festus who were sitting on the porch. Clara brought out a pitcher of iced tea as the day had warmed up some.

Sarah asked Clara, "Do you think we can take time today and go on a picnic?"

"I think we can, there's nothing so pressing that we can't take a few hours and go out by the stream. Let me put together something for a picnic basket and we'll go," she answered.

Sarah stepped up on the porch and turned to the boys saying, "I'll just give her a hand and we can go that much sooner. Can you hook up that bay horse to our buckboard while we're getting things ready?"

"Be happy to," Willy said.

The two ladies went inside to prepare the picnic basket (and themselves) for their afternoon with their two gentlemen callers. The McCoys looked around the ranch from where they were on the porch and could tell that it was a place that was well-cared for and well-run. They headed toward the barn to find the buckboard and they hooked up the horse. Finishing their appointed chore, they pulled the buckboard around to the front of the house. The ladies came out with the picnic basket and said they could all ride in the buckboard.

The McCoys, feeling nervous about leaving their horses, asked if they could just tie the reins to the back of the small wagon and bring their horses with them.

Clara nodded and Willy was glad she understood how most men felt about their horses, especially in an unfamiliar place.

"Of course," she said.

Festus and Sarah sat in the back and Clara and Willy sat on the bench and drove the wagon. The McCoys commented on how nice of a ranch they had and what beautiful country surrounded them. It took about 20 minutes to get to the stream and a few more to arrive at the beautiful, grassy area. They untied their horses and let them graze, leaving the bay attached to the buggy. The women laid the blanket out and set the picnic basket on it. They sat down and looked up at the clear sky and the big clouds blowing around.

Clara said, "Who would like to go for a walk?"

Willy said he would, but the other two declined.

When they left, Clara hooked her arm in the crook of Willy's elbow.

"So, tell me all about yourself," she asked.

Willy told her where the family came from. Then he said, "We all joined up for the war and after the war we tried to work a ranch near Lawrence, but a few of us got itchy feet and we left."

He was careful to leave out the part about the raids and the gold they had, and he hoped Festus would do the same. Willy recounted some details about his childhood, and where they were from and how their families were no longer there—at least they never got any reply from the letters they sent—and that they had no idea where the rest of the family was or how to contact them.

"So, we're starting a new life on our own with some of our other kinfolk that had been on the ranch."

Clara took her arm away from Willy's elbow and grasped his hand while she leaned up against the tree that seemed to be placed there just for her to lean on. Drawing him close to her she put her arms around his neck and kissed him lovingly. Willy had no idea this would happen, and he felt he was in a dreamlike trance, just following along with what she wanted. Of course, kissing was something he wanted himself, but he'd had no idea how he was going to get to that point. Luckily for him, this was a woman who knew what she wanted and had no problems about showing him. Best of all, instead of feeling threatened by it, like he knew some men might have, he saw it as a strength that she would be the one to kiss him. They could have some fun together in the backcountry, riding and shooting and hunting. It was a match made in heaven as far as he was concerned.

After a while, Clara said, "Let's go see what we put in the picnic basket."

As they arrived back at the blanket, Sarah and Festus arrived too.

"Ah, here they are. Where'd you two head off to?" Clara asked.

It was Festus who answered. "We decided to take a nice walk along the creek."

The two couples enjoyed the sandwiches Clara had put together. Afterward, they walked down to the stream where the ladies took off their boots and walked barefoot just inside the edge of the water while the men searched the shore for skipping stones. After a while, Sarah suggested they head back to the ranch, as they needed to prepare supper for the ranch hands. Willy could have stayed there for much longer, and though he knew that running a ranch was a lot of work, he wouldn't have minded one more kiss.

When they reached the ranch, one of the ranch hands came up to the buckboard and said he would take care of it. The ladies climbed down and all four went up on the porch. Sarah and Clara thanked the men for their visit and said they would like them to come back again soon.

The McCoys stood with their hats in their hands.

Festus said, "It was our pleasure to visit."

Willy said, "We hope that we can come to see you ladies again very soon."

"You boys are proper gentlemen and we're proper ladies, but you best be careful," said Sarah. "We've got some wildcat in us too. You think you might be up to the challenge?"

Clara laughed at her sister and poked her with her elbow.

The men laughed, too. Festus said, "I know I'd sure like to try. I've never met a woman like you, Sarah, and don't think I ever will again."

Sarah blushed. Quickly Clara said, "How would you boys like to come over for Sunday dinner?"

Festus responded, "We'd like that very much, and I'm sure interested in seeing how your cook'n is, seeing how everything else has been perfect."

"Then I guess we'll see you Sunday, have a nice evening, boys," Clara said.

Willy and Festus mounted their horses and waved to the two ladies as they stood on the porch. Willy watched them go inside, Clara the last one in.

"I can't believe our good fortune," said Festus.

"Me either," said Willy in a rather serious tone.

They turned the horses toward the ranch and headed home.

...

The rest of the days in the week seemed to take forever to pass and get to Sunday for the two McCoys. When it finally arrived, they were ready to go by 9 a.m. and were trying to find ways to kill time. They couldn't show up too early. They decided to go into town while waiting until noon before they left. They rode slowly and talked.

Festus was always the first to talk when it came to the ladies. "I wouldn't mind startin' a family with Sarah," he said.

"Me neither," said Willy. Then quickly added. "With Clara, that is."

"But how do we explain the gold?"

"What do you think they would think about us?" Festus asked.

"I guess that depends on what we say and how we say it."

"I don't know, Festus. We sure can't lie. Can we?"

Festus shrugged, looking worried.

While they were in town, they stopped to buy some cider and, it being winter, they had to settle for chocolates instead of flowers. Festus found a nice block of cheese and some freshly made butter and Willy picked up some dried lavender for the fire.

They arrived about 1:30 and Sarah and Clara emerged from the house wearing Sunday dresses, smiling radiantly at them as they stepped up on the porch.

Willy was greeted with a kiss and, he noticed, so was

Festus. Willy wondered what the ladies said about them when they talked among themselves and he hoped it was all good. Clara accepted the gifts and said, "The lavender is so thoughtful. Thank you."

"Why don't you go and put your horses in the corral and let them run free," Sarah said.

The McCoys did as they were told and returned to the house. They stood outside for a moment. Festus reached for the door handle, but Willy batted his hand away.

"We should knock," Willy said.

Clara opened the door. "Please come in gentlemen and make yourselves at home, "We'll be right with you, we just have a couple of things to finish in the kitchen."

Stepping inside, they couldn't help but notice what a nice well-kept home it was. As they walked around admiring the place, they were impressed by the furniture and the elegant objects resting on pedestals and the fireplace mantle. There was a full-size sofa and a beautiful settee with a matching set of armchairs facing the fireplace. In the direction of the kitchen (from which wafted the delectable scents of a hearty supper), there was a large open area where they spotted a cherry wood dining table that could sit 8 to 10 people easily. Several paintings spread out along the walls and in the far end of the room there was a roll-top desk and chair that was backed by an extensive library.

"There must be a hundred books," said Festus.

"I'm feeling a little bit out of place," said Willy, thinking these ladies were raised in elegance and were probably book smart.

"I don't know, though," said Willy. "They sure don't act like they're snobs."

"I never saw that with them. They seem like down home people to me," said Festus.

When Sarah returned to the living area, she noticed they hadn't sat down.

"Please have a seat," she said.

"I don't know where to sit," Willy said. "Your house is so nice, I'm afraid I might get something dirty if I sit on it."

"Oh please, these are old things passed down for generations. Our father left all of it to us and we use them the same as you would any furniture in your house, so please get comfortable." She said.

Clara came in and wiping her hands on her apron, she said, "We're just like anyone else, just plain country folk. Don't judge us by what my father tried to appear to be. If this wasn't already here when we took over, we'd be sitting on plank benches and eating on pine tabletops."

"To be honest, plank benches and pine tabletops are more our style," Festus said.

"Well good then, we should get along just fine," said Clara.

A gentle laughter rolled through all four of them, and the men felt more at ease, but still sat in the wooden chairs at the dining table.

Clara excused herself saying she'd be back in a moment.

Sarah then asked, "I hope you boys don't have a

problem about drinking coffee in the afternoon, because I sure would like to have a cup. I just finished boiling some. Any takers?"

Both of the McCoys said they would, and that they enjoyed a good cup of coffee anytime. Just then Clara came out of the kitchen. She was carrying a tray with four tin cups and a coffeepot.

Clara poured the coffee and Sarah suggested that they take their coffee out on the porch where they had a nice swing bench and a couple of chairs.

"We can enjoy this sun while we have it," Clara said

The four of them spent the next hour chatting. The women talked about how they had a lot of work on their ranch.

"I feel like we are always trying to catch up," Sarah said.

"We don't have too much to do on our ranch," said Festus.

Willy nodded his head. He was thinking how much better it would be if they had more work. But they weren't planning on staying very long either. Still, the winter wasn't even half over, and he was a little bored.

"We were going to try our luck in the gold fields in Colorado or the Dakota Territories, but the more we think about it, the more we don't know what we want to do," said Willy.

"We were hoping we could get rich in gold and then settle down on a ranch raising horses and cattle," Festus said.

Both women could not hide their surprise.

"Are you leaving then?" said Sarah. She seemed disappointed.

"Well..." Willy said, "Now that we've met you two..."

"It seemed like this week would never end and Sunday just wasn't going to come," said Festus. "I don't think I've passed a longer week ever, not even in the war."

The ladies blushed a little and Clara spoke, "Well, the truth be told, we've been quite anxious all week ourselves."

Sarah said, "We were hoping nothing would come up that would delay or cancel your visit today."

A calm feeling came over them.

Clara stood up. "I hope you like what we've put together for dinner, it's one of our favorites too, and both of us know how to cook."

"Speaking of cooking, the bread should be ready about now. I'm going to go check on it," Sarah said. While the bread cooled, Clara and Sarah put the dishes on the table and the two McCoys finished their coffee on the porch.

After a short while, Clara called them to the table and once seated they were pleasantly surprised to see that they were going to be served, just like they were served at home growing up. They remembered how all the plates were at one end of the table and all of the food close to that end, where their mother dished up the portions. Sarah carved the roast beef and Clara put the mashed potatoes and green beans that they had canned earlier in the year on their plates. They covered the potatoes in the beef gravy and put a slice of corn bread on their plates. After they were served, they put their plates on the table in front of a chair and waited for the ladies to load up their plates. Finally, they all sat down.

The two ladies looked at the men slightly embarrassed, and Clara asked if they minded if they said grace.

Festus replied, "This feels so much like my own home when I was growing up, we always used to say grace too, please do."

Clara began: "Thank you Lord, for the food we are about to receive to nourish our bodies and thank you for the company of these two nice gentleman and bringing them into our lives, in Jesus' name, amen."

The food was excellent, everything cooked just perfectly. Willy was impressed by these two beautiful women and their abilities. Not only could they run a ranch, but they could cook and ride and shoot like champs. After the long repast, they leaned back in their chairs.

"Willy," said Clara. "Would you put a log on the fireplace."

"Yes," he said.

He noticed there were only a couple of logs by the fireplace, so he went outside to the woodshed that was beside the house and picked up an arm full and brought the wood back in. Feeling how cold it was outside, he did this twice more to make sure the ladies had plenty of wood in the house for the evening and the morning. He wanted to remember to do the same thing before they left, so they had wood close by for the next few days. Once the fire was lit, and the house warm, the room felt very cozy. Clara asked if they would like some hot cider, saying she liked to drink hot cider on cold nights. All were in agreement that it was a good idea. When they all had their cups of hot cider and were sitting in front of the fireplace, they heard the wind pick up outside.

Sarah stood up and looked out the window. "Storm's a coming," she said. "You should put your horses in the barn before it gets worse outside."

The men hurried to take care of their animals and get them shelter. While getting the horses, it began to rain, then very quickly turned into sleet.

"I hope it don't snow," said Festus. "It sure feels cold."

Willy didn't say anything. With the blowing wind, the rain cut right through and chilled him to the bone. By the time they got back inside the house, they were both shivering. The two ladies fetched blankets for them to wrap up in while sitting in front of the fireplace.

Clara said, "I think you had best stay the night here, it's getting bad outside, and we don't know how long it's going to stay that way. I sure don't want you out in this weather trying to make it home. Besides we have four bedrooms here and lots of blankets."

"Oh, we've been in weather worse than this and

didn't have any blankets either, we'll be okay riding home," Festus said,

Hearing this, Willy wanted to say something. He couldn't believe Festus wanted to show how rugged they were, rather than realize what had been offered. When Festus looked over at Willy, he gave him Festus a look. Only then did Festus understand his mistake.

"We won't take no for answer," said Clara. "It can get very bad, maybe even snow. Would you rather us worry all night wonderin' if you made it back home safely?"

"Listen to that wind. I suspect the snow will come shortly," said Sarah.

They agreed to stay the night. The four of them sat close to the fire. Willy realized he hadn't felt so relaxed in years, and after the hearty meal and drinking the hot cider, it wasn't long before he dozed off. He didn't know that they had all fallen asleep.

Clara was the first to wake, feeling a chill because the fire had died down. She realized she had fallen asleep, as had her sister. She got out from under the blanket and added a couple of small logs to the fire. She inadvertently woke Willy while doing this and he said softly, "So where are we going to sleep tonight?"

At the sound of his voice, the other two started stirring under their blanket and waking up. Clara took his hand and pulled him to his feet. She lit an oil lamp sitting on the shelf by the table saying, "Come along, I'll show you."

Not letting go of his hand, she led him down the

hallway. There were two doors on each side of the hallway marking the entrances to the bedrooms. She went to the second set of doors, stopped in front of the one on the left and said, "This is where you will be sleeping. My room is right across the hall."

She opened the door and walked in while saying, "I'll just pull out the blankets from the closet for you."

As she did so, Willy looked around at the modest furnishings in comparison to the living area. The room was comfortable looking with a nice chest of drawers, a wardrobe and a table next to the bed with a lamp. He noticed there was a Bible on the table next to a candle. Clara set two blankets on a chair and spread a comforter over the bedspread. She then went to one corner up by the pillows and pulled the covers back so that it was ready to climb into. When she looked up to see him gazing at her and smiling, she blushed slightly and said, "Those two blankets on the chair are in case the comforter is not enough. I'll be right across the hall if you need anything or get scared of the lightning and thunder."

They both laughed as she winked at him. Then she grew more serious. "Sometimes Sarah gets afraid when storms are bad and sleeps with me. Having someone to hold on to when it's storming outside really is comforting."

He didn't get the subtle invitation right away.

"The weather doesn't scare me. If cannons and explosions going off around me didn't stop me from being able to sleep, I don't think lightning and thunder will be a problem," Willy said. He wanted her to know that maybe one day, he could be the one by her side when she was scared. Then he realized what she had meant and wanted to kick himself.

"Okay then, get yourself a good night's rest," she responded. She usually spoke her mind clearly when she had something to say or wanted someone to know something, but she felt she needed to be a little discrete under these romantic circumstances. As she came out of the room and entered hers across the hall, she saw Festus and Sarah walking down the hallway. She waved and said good night and so did they.

Sarah did the same thing for Festus in his room, only when she was finished, she walked up very close to him and said, "Have a good night's sleep and sweet dreams of me. I'll be right across the hall if you need anything." She tilted her face upward and leaned in to give him a lingering kiss. She took her hands away from his chest, blinking and smiling at him.

"Good night," she said. She winked, and he thought she swiveled her hips as she walked through the door and then closed it. Festus wasn't sure what to make of it, but he was sure what he wanted it to mean. But now, he didn't know what he should be doing. He thought for a while and then sat down and took his boots off. Deciding to go ahead and be the gentleman, and not try to see something extra in her actions or in his wishful imagination, he undressed. As he climbed into bed, he couldn't stop thinking about the way she acted. After several minutes of deliberating, he told himself that if he misunderstood her actions as an invitation, he could simply go back to his room and go to sleep. As he stood up to get dressed, there was a loud crackling and a thunderous boom of lightning that shook the floor and walls of the house. Making his way to the door and stepping into the hallway, another heavy thunder bolt sounded outside. Just as he was about to knock, the door opened and there she stood in her night gown and shawl, looking frightened.

Startled by him being there when she opened the door, she put her hand to her chest exclaiming, "Oh my, you startled me. I didn't expect you to be right here. I get scared sometimes when the thunder and lightning is so loud and close. I don't like to be alone while it's going on."

Festus felt he had to explain what he was doing at her door, "I was just coming to see about that. I wouldn't want you to be alone and afraid, when I'm right here and able to help you feel safe."

"Well, let's not just stand here in the hallway, come in. I am a little scared and now I'm also cold being out from under my blankets."

As he stepped into her room and she climbed back into her bed underneath the covers, he realized he was standing there in his long Johns and was embarrassed, not knowing what to say about his appearance. She could tell he was uncomfortable and said, "I've seen men in their long johns before, so don't be embarrassed and don't stand there in the cold, get in here under the covers."

He did not hesitate and was quickly by her side under the covers in her bed.

At the time of those loud thunderclaps, Willy was thinking about what Clara had said. He got up his courage and went out into the hallway to knock on her door, barely missing the scene between Sarah and Festus.

He tapped lightly on the door and as Clara opened it, they looked at each other for a long moment, and then came together in a long kiss. When they pulled away, she opened the door wider and stepped aside, motioning with her hand for him to come inside. She closed the door, went to the bed and flipped back the covers, then took his hand as she climbed in the bed saying, "Come on, get in here."

He didn't say a word, just did as he was told. In the dark, helped by the light of the moon through the window he saw that her room was neat and feminine, with a pretty vanity and mirror, and some lace curtains and flowered wallpaper. She had a woodstove for warmth and the room was nice and comfortable.

The next morning the ladies woke up early, as was their custom on the ranch and went to the kitchen to prepare breakfast. Willy woke as Clara left the room, realizing his clothes were in the room across the hall. Festus also must have realized this too because when Willy opened the door to look out into the hallway, he found himself looking at Festus's head sticking out of the doorway to Sarah's room. They smiled at each other and quickly stepped out into the hall and closed the door behind them quietly, then stealthily snuck into their own rooms to get dressed.

After they dressed, Willy and Festus met each other in the hallway and exchanged dumbfounded expressions and a couple of words before heading for breakfast. Willy noticed both he and Festus seemed surprised and happy, but also slightly disappointed in what happened the night before. For Willy and Festus, it seemed clear that Clara and Sara actually only wanted company to keep them warm and feel safe, because all they did was snuggle up and fall asleep quickly. But then Willy realized that he really just wanted to be a gentleman anyway and wouldn't have felt right had it been any other way.

"That's a night to remember for me," said, Willy. "She's a woman to respect."

"Me, too," said Festus. "I agree."

"I'm just glad I got to be by her side."

"Me, too," said Festus.

After their conversation, they headed to the dining table and everyone said good morning to each other. The ladies handed Willy and Festus a cup of coffee and told them to have a seat at the table. Willy went to the fireplace and he noticed there were still enough coals to get the fire started and got the fire going again. Looking outside he saw a fine layer of snow and the cold barren trees. The women had cooked a massive amount of scrambled eggs, potatoes and bacon. They piled one large skillet high with all of the food, and they left to give the ranch hands their breakfast. When the woman returned, they served breakfast, which was another mouthwatering meal. The two McCoys were so smitten with the Braxton sisters that they didn't want to leave, but knew they needed to.

After breakfast, they went to the barn and saddled their horses, bringing them over to the hitching post in front of the house. The two sisters insisted they have one more cup of coffee for the road, so they once again sat out on the front porch and enjoyed a cup of coffee with the two ladies and the sun rose high. It was cold but they were all dressed warmly, and Willy felt warm from the kindness of the two ladies and the hearty breakfast they served.

When they all had finished their coffee, Sarah stood and said, "We need to see what kind of damages been done around the ranch from that storm. Clara we have work to do."

"We should be doing the same back at our place," said Willy. "But if you don't mind, we'd like to drop by when we get some more free time, if it's okay with you?"

"You boys are welcome any time you feel like coming by," said Clara looking mainly at Willy. "And be careful get'n home."

"It's been real nice being here with you and I can't say as when I've passed a better stormy night," said Festus.

They all stood and the McCoys walked down the porch steps to their horses and mounted up. As they turned their horses towards the road, they both tipped the front of their hats with their fingers giving the ladies a respectful nod. Willy yelled out as they started down the road, "We'll be back soon, you can count on it."

CHAPTER 18

WHAT TO DO ABOUT THE GOLD

Willy and Festus had been back two days from visiting the Braxton sisters, when Sam and William made it back to the ranch. James was in the house and Junior was dumping a bucket of dishwater as they came onto the property. Junior went up on the porch and started clanging the "come and get it" triangle they used to announce dinner was ready or if something important was going on at the main house. When the others heard it, they knew they needed to come quickly.

Sam and William dismounted and sat down on the porch waiting for the others to gather around. After everyone was present, they went through their ordeal, recounting as much of the details as they could remember. The meaning of this disaster put a chill through all of the McCoys. Now, they were all afraid of where they were planning to go in the spring, wondering if this was how the traveling would be. They spoke their turns, wondering things like whether they would even get there and whether it was worth taking the risk.

Sam was still recovering from his shoulder wound and would probably be a few more weeks convalescing. They offered him a bunk to stay on the ranch so he wouldn't have to pay for a hotel and would have some help if he needed any. He was much obliged and accepted their offer.

First thing the following morning William took the gold he brought back with him out where he had stashed it before he left. He spent some time digging a new hole and buried it, throwing rocks and topsoil on top to make it look like nothing at all was buried there. For the next few days there was a heavy somber air around the ranch as each McCoy mourned the loss of their kinfolk once again. They all had doubts over whether leaving the ranch near Lawrence had been a good idea for those of them that were left. They knew it had been a disastrous choice for those they had lost.

Festus and Willy talked among themselves and decided they wanted to ask the Braxton sisters to marry them.

"It sounds safer anyway than heading west," said Willy.

Festus nodded. It was clear they were both sad about the loss but also eager to move on with their lives.

"I'll bring it up when the time seems right," said Willy.

Willy could not get the thought of Clara out of his

mind. He knew Festus was the same. It was all he thought about. He saw how hard the women worked and knew they could use help. And he now realized, as he and Festus had discussed, it was more than just lending the ladies a hand. They would ask them for their hand in marriage when it seemed right.

He and Festus had gone out to the ranch a couple of times and hinted to the women that they would like to come out and help on the ranch while they waited for winter to pass. On their last visit, both sisters decided they would like to have their company on the ranch.

"It would be good to have your help and you already know where your bedrooms are," Sarah said.

"We don't mind what people might say, let them think what they want," said Clara "But what Sarah means is we are okay with you staying in the main house as long as you stay in the guestrooms."

One evening back at the McCoy ranch while having their dinner, Festus and Willy decided to tell the others what they had in mind.

Willy spoke to his kin first, "I know, y'all know we've been seeing the Braxton sisters, only now for us it's gotten serious. We're thinking we'd like to marry these gals and start a family with them on their ranch. We thought we'd ask your opinions on it, if you thought we were far enough away from Lawrence to be safe, or if we would be putting them in needless danger, just being selfish of our own desires."

Jonesy was the first to speak. "Y'all know that it's still dangerous for all of us, having that gold around and anyone around us would be suspected also, if we're caught. As far as being far enough away, I think there's plenty of distance between us and the ranch, but if word gets out that we were the ones that pulled off those raids, wherever any McCoys are they will be under suspicion until they can show they were not part of those raids. So here is just as good as anywhere else and if you found love for yourselves, I say lucky you, and do your best for those ladies."

Festus and Willy remained quiet, listening.

"You need to decide if you want to try to use that gold or just be rid of it and live off what you can create at the ranch they have," Billy piped in. "Plus, you have to be darn sure those ladies won't go to the sheriff after you tell them about the gold."

Willy spoke up with his thoughts about the gold. "I think we can take our gold down to the stream they have on the property and bury it, then after some time, we can dig it up and melt it down like Wiley did, setting up a sluice box in the stream to claim that's where we found it."

Jonesy responded, "That's a pretty good plan, but have you thought about what those women will think about you having that gold? Or are you going to hide that fact from them and make them think you actually found gold in the stream, never telling them where it really came from. I know from experience when things are hidden from people and they find the truth out later, it can completely ruin your relationship with them, even if it didn't harm them directly.

Billy interrupted. "With women, they want to know the truth about a man's past up front, before they devote their futures to them, and they expect their men to be honest about it. I realize it's going to be hard to make this here decision for you, but you need to think it out all the way, and not just hope ever'thing just works out all right.

That got Festus and Willy pondering heavily what they should do.

After a few minutes of everyone eating and Willy thinking things through, Billy continued. "I can tell you this; trying to keep that gold is not worth your life, but it sure would make for a nice life if you could use it. I think what every man is looking for is a woman he can love and trust, and it's the same for women. So, if your heart has found what it truly wants and its place is in their heart and most importantly, they feel the same, then you should tell them the truth and let them help you decide what you should do with the gold." He paused, picked something out of his teeth then said, with a sly smile. "You can let them know that you have no problem with leaving it with us to divide up amongst ourselves."

Everyone laughed, then Billy went on, "I'm not saying this because I want your gold, I'm just saying this is the right thing to do. If you decide not to keep it, I'm sure those of us that are going to keep ours, won't care if we have more. Then you won't have the problem of what you're going to do with it."

The other McCoys around the table nodded and

Junior said, "That's right, what you should do is be honest all the way through and let them decide about you and the gold, knowing everything at the start."

Everyone at the table nodded and a few of them said things like, "That's the right thing to do."

So now Festus and Willy had their family's opinion to help them decide and both of them agreed with the group consensus, deciding to go out to the ranch the next morning and tell the truth to the ladies, risking their hearts and future with them, not to mention their freedom if the ladies went to the sheriff. Something told Willy they would never do that, and Festus said, "It's the right thing to do, even if they do tell the sheriff." The next morning, they rode out to where they had hidden their gold, dug it up and went together to see Sarah and Clara, taking their wagons and gold with them.

CHAPTER 19

SHERIFF DODD AND
THE PINKERTONS

That same morning, Agent Tucker and his group of Pinkerton agents rode into town. Slim had hoped that on their journey he was going to get an opportunity to get away. He knew sitting in jail where they caught him gave him no chance to escape and he knew what was coming to him, if they left him there. He even took them to the exact spot in the road where the ambush took place, hoping they might take the handcuffs off him at some point, and he might get a chance to run off and hide. That never happened.

Agent Tucker wasn't about to risk him getting away. They kept him tied up, a rope around his waist and tied to his saddle, with another one tied to his ankles going under the belly of his horse and handcuffed the entire time they traveled, except when they stopped to sleep. Then they untied the ropes attached to the saddle and his ankles, but subsequently tied him up to a tree or two saddles together, if no trees were around.

Arriving at the Sheriff's office, agent Tucker went inside pulling a handcuffed Slim with him. The Sheriff was at his desk, and as he looked up, he recognized Slim as the one described by the McCoys who had brought the fake Dusty Trails to them and had organized the guiding of the McCoys and the ambush.

He smiled and said, "Well looky here, if it ain't the thief and bushwhacker I've been looking to find for almost a month now."

The Sheriff had been keeping tabs on the McCoys and had learned they were an honest and good group of men. He also knew that they had another group of their kinfolk join them at the ranch. What he didn't know was that three of them had tried to brave the elements and get to Deadwood in the winter, only to have two more of them get killed. After hearing what the Sheriff said about Slim, agent Tucker introduced himself.

"Hello Sheriff, I'm Capt. Tucker, head agent of a group of Pinkerton agents."

The Sheriff also introduced himself and offered his hand to shake hands with Capt. Tucker. "I'm Sheriff Dodd. How can I help you?"

"We've been scouring the country for some missing gold coins," said Agent Tucker. "We've been following up on the reports wherever they've been turning up. Then we ran into this polecat, who said he could identify the men he took the wagons from and that the gold was in it when they stole the wagons." Explained agent Tucker.

The Sheriff seemed astonished. "What gold are you

talking about?" he asked. "I know the fellas that were robbed, three of them got killed when it happened, and they all seem to be good people. You're taking the word of a thief and bushwhacker as gospel? Can't say as I'd do that, not without proof. I haven't seen or heard anything about any gold since they've been here." Agent Tucker couldn't believe his ears when he heard that the ones that had the gold were still in the area.

"Who are they and where are they. I need to get to them right away?" Asked Tucker.

"Well, that'd be the McCoys. They're staying out on a ranch about five miles outside of town, wait'n for the winter to be over so they can head on to Denver or Deadwood, at least that's what they told me."

Hearing the name "McCoy," the old suspicion that he had in Lawrence about them was quickly revived. Although hearing the sheriff speak well of them, made him think he may have put too much stock in what Slim had said. Possibly Tucker just wanted it to be true too much, so he wasn't thinking rationally. Then again, maybe he was actually going to get to the bottom of this.

"I can take you out there, if you'd like?" The Sheriff said. He wanted to go along because this didn't sound like the McCoys he knew, and he wanted to be there if anything happened.

Agent Tucker looked at Slim and said, "I'd like to go just as soon as you take this thief and now it seems, also a murderer, and put him in a cell.

The sheriff took care of locking the man up in the cell in the back of his office. It was roughly 10 a.m.

when the Sheriff rode out with agent Tucker and the two other Pinkerton agents to visit the McCoys. The other three agents that were supposed to meet agent Tucker there in Kansas City, still had a two-day ride before they arrived.

When they got to the ranch, Sheriff Dodd asked agent Tucker and his men to wait on their horses while he went up and knocked on the door. James answered the door. He'd been preparing some food for the rest of the McCoys who were out doing chores around the ranch. Agent Tucker hadn't met any of the other McCoys previously, except for Tommy and his dad; Thomas, Sr., so he didn't know if they even knew he had been out to the ranch asking questions.

The Sheriff and James exchanged greetings. Then the Sheriff said, "The Pinkertons captured Slim and he's sitting in my jail right now."

James nodded, trying not to relive that terrible day.

He said, "Those men over there are the ones that captured Slim, and they are Pinkerton agents who've been following a trail of gold coins for quite some time. They'd like to ask you some questions."

"Sure," said James. "If there's anything we can do to help, we'd be glad to."

The Sheriff motioned for the Pinkertons to come up on the porch. When they stepped up on the porch, Sheriff Dodd introduced agent Tucker as Capt. Tucker and the other two as deputies.

Agent Tucker took no time with niceties. "Are you part of the group of McCoys who were working the ranch down around Lawrence, Kansas?" He asked.

Right away, James knew he had to be careful how he answered. Looking agent Tucker direct in the eye, he responded. "We sure are. Why are you wondering about that?"

"Well, being in this line of work for so long, coincidences are not very often just coincidences. It seems that several times when we've come across the stolen gold coins, some McCoys from that ranch had something to do with the people we found that had the coins," agent Tucker explained.

"I can assure you none of the McCoys on that ranch have anything to do with any stolen gold coins." James said. In reality this wasn't a lie; they had taken the gold coins from the northern Army's soldiers who had stolen them from the Northern Army, after the armies raiding groups had stolen them from the southern people. It was their reward for getting it back.

"If you think we might have some gold on us, you're more than welcome to look around. We got nothin' to hide. We all got some money from Wiley, who struck it rich when he got home to Pikeville after he left the ranch in Lawrence. He wanted us to all have a chance to start our lives over after the war, so he staked us all a little over $3000 each to get us a good start. Of course, we'll all have to pay him back, which was part of the deal he made us. All of us still have most everything he sent us, hope'n to wait out the winter here. That's how we're able to live now, since the ranch was unable to pay us for work'n there. Try'n it ourselves on our own land didn't work out so well either. Most of us thought we would move on while we had us a good grub stake."

Agent Tucker listened to what James was saying and remembered that they did all get money from the one that went home to Kentucky. "When would be a good time for everyone bein' around so I can talk to all of you and get to see who everyone is?"

"Sunday would be the best day," James said. "Why don't you come by for Sunday dinner here with us?"

Agent Tucker thought that would be just fine with him. Being a few days away, it would give his other agents time to join him. But being Captain Tucker of the Pinkerton detective agency, he knew when he came upon somebody by surprise, they didn't have time to hide things that they might want to remain unseen.

"That sounds like a great idea, but I'd like to take you up on your offer of letting me look around, just the same, if you don't mind."

"Sure, go right ahead. Make yourself at home, anywhere you want to look, just don't go tearing up the place while you're looking around. I have to get back inside since I got stuff to do in the kitchen," James said.

James then went back inside the house and Sheriff Dodd and agent Tucker looked at each other. Sheriff Dodd felt content that he'd been right about these McCoys because he was thinking that if they were guilty of anything, they surely wouldn't be letting agent Tucker walk around the ranch looking for evidence against them. Agent Tucker told his deputies to come look around with him in the barn and the corral to see if they could find anything useful to confirm his suspicions. When they finished looking in the barn and around the corral and found no indication of anything out of place or suspicious, agent Tucker decided they would just go back to town and wait for his other deputies to show up. Then they'd all come back on Sunday.

CHAPTER 20

TRUTH TELLING

Festus and Willy were nervous on their ride to the Braxton ranch, unsure of their fates with the two women they were in love with. When they arrived, they parked their wagons over by the barn and left them covered with their tarps. They unhitched their horses and let them loose in the corral. They walked the long walk to the steps of the main house, which actually was a short distance, but seemed like a walk to the gallows. The two sisters hadn't heard them drive by the house with their wagons as they were busy inside the house with the chores. After knocking on the door, Sarah opened it, happily surprised, it seemed, to see the two McCoys standing there.

Smiling she said, "You boys seem to always make it here just in time for a meal. You must really like our cooking."

Festus and Willy laughed.

"Come on in and we'll set you a place at the table. We were just about to eat ourselves," Sarah said.

Festus and Willy both thought it would be best if

they had a nice lunch first, before they let the cat out of the bag.

The sisters served a roast chicken and potatoes. The two men had coffee and enjoyed the delicious meal. After eating, the sisters once again offered hot cider and a comfortable seat out on the porch.

"Did you bring your things to move into your bedrooms?" Sarah asked.

"We did, but before we do that, we think you need to know something more about us."

The two women seemed alarmed.

Willy cleared his throat and said, "We think you know we came from mountain and hill people that were not very well off, fairly poor actually. But also, none of us ever went past the sixth grade in school. When we got to be 12 years old, we were needed to either hunt or work in the logging business that our family did to bring in money."

"I admire men who know the gifts of hard work and sacrifice," Sarah said softly.

"That's how we grew up and then came the war," Festus said. "Every male over 14 had to join the fight. So, we fought for the south, which was where we came from and the side our family chose. We hope you won't hold that against us, because we are still honest and good people. We believe a man's word is his honor and that we should do onto others as they had done unto us. We also grew up with the idea that family and neighbors help each other whenever possible, or when someone is in need of help, and we should not expect payment for it. We're not afraid of hard work and know that things don't just happen, you need to work to make them happen, and having a home or ranch and family takes hard work and is worth working for."

The women nodded. Clara said, "We were worried but so far, everything you've said aligns with our values."

Willy frowned and took over. "We also believe that if we know that a wrong has been done to someone and we can fix it or somehow make it right, then we should do that, if it's within our capability."

"Sounds like you had some good upbringing," Sarah said.

"I believe your family had good morals," Clara said. "Seems ya'll believe in helping thy neighbor, which is also the way we were taught."

"That brings us to what we want to tell you the most," said Festus. "When we surrendered at the end of the war, a group of us McCoys met in a little valley a short ways away from Fort Scott where we surrendered. We all had heard the rumors about the North raiding towns and plantations all along the Missouri border and further south into Tennessee and other parts. We'd been told they were stealing everything and killing most everyone they stole it from. Sometimes they let them live, but they burned down their houses and took everything of value. We heard stories of these huge stockpiles of southern valuables being kept in different places along the Missouri-Kansas border. One of our kinfolk managed to get some detailed information about where these stockpiles were. Our group that met over by Fort Scott decided we were going to try to take back those valuables stolen from the southern people even though the war was over.

Willy took over. "We were among the first to surrender and it was going to take a few weeks for all the surrendering to get completed since there were so many soldiers spread out across the country. The North wanted the southern soldiers to report to specific areas close to where they had been fighting and turn in their weapons and flags, not to mention horses and anything else they had in their possession. Once we did that, we were free to go, but all we had were the clothes on our backs. Some of us were smart enough to stash a few weapons and horses in the woodland areas close by to where we had to surrender and went back and recovered them, once we were released to go home."

"To make a long story short," Festus said. "We joined together, 22 of us in all, all McCoys. We decided even if we lost the war, we were going to try to do something right for the South. So, we went after those stockpiles of valuables and succeeded in taking a lot of it back. It was in the form of household items that were valuable, and guns. There were also many strong boxes full of gold coins. We took the most part of it to a preacher in Harrisonville, who between his church and the mayor gave it back to those in need and set up many programs for people to rebuild their lives without having to pay back the money. They also rebuilt their town.

Willy looked at the faces of Sarah and Clara while

Festus paused. He couldn't tell what they were thinking. He said, "We didn't want to be going home empty-handed and broke, so we decided we would keep for ourselves a small portion of it, and everyone in our group got the same amount of gold from what we had taken back from the north, and we kept it for ourselves. We still have our share of the gold, but we can't spend it the way it is because it's in fifty-dollar gold pieces. There is a general in Independence, Missouri who was the leader of those from the north who were raiding the groups in the south, and he instructed the leaders of the groups that he commanded to keep a portion of everything they plundered from the southern people for themselves and required them to give a percentage of it to him. At the end of the war, they were supposed to have turned over everything to the military, like they were supposed to have been doing all along to finance the war and then those that didn't want to stay in the military could go home."

The women were listening carefully. Now they both nodded as Willy continued, "The leaders of the groups under the general's command didn't turn in everything they were supposed to and that's where all of these valuables and gold came from. These were things that they had kept for themselves, hiding it from the military so that when they discharged out of their units, they were going to be rich. The Northern military knows nothing about this gold except for the general and those leaders of the northern raiding groups. They are what is known as war criminals for taking advantage of their position and jobs during the war for personal gain. What we did was, we took from them what they had stolen from the Northern Army, who had originally taken it from the Southern people."

"That's some way to make a long story short," said Festus. "What he's trying to say is that this general hired the Pinkertons to look for the gold that was taken without telling them where it originated from, or the fact that he had stolen it from the Army. So, there are Pinkerton agents running all over Missouri looking for this gold, thinking it was stolen from the Army. That's why we can't use it the way it is, in the form of those coins. We'll have to melt it down and turn it into an assayer's office in order to claim it as our own. We'll have to make it look like we found it in the ground and file a mining claim. That's if we want to keep it."

Both men looked at Clara and Sarah. Hearts beating nervously, they waited for the women to say something, but nothing was forthcoming. Willy couldn't read Clara's face, but he was sure she was disgusted with him. When he looked at Sarah, he noticed her frowning. He and Festus looked at each other. They knew it was the end of their relationships. But at least they'd been honest. And that counted for something.

The two sisters, hands clasped together in front of them, looked shocked.

Willy stood up. Festus did the same. So convinced were they that the two women had changed their minds about them that they put their hats on.

Willy said, "We understand, ladies. And we will take

our leave. We hope you can find it in your hearts to forgive us. And maybe you could keep it from Sheriff Dodd."

Festus nodded. "But we will understand if you feel you need to tell him."

Clara and Sarah looked at each other.

"Sorry to disappoint you," Willy said as he and Festus started to walk back to their wagon.

Then Clara said, "Well, hold on a minute."

"For heaven's sake," said Sarah. "Come back here and sit down."

"It's a lot to take in, boys, but we aren't sending you away," said Clara, smiling.

Festus broke out into a grin. Willy said, "You're not?"

Then Sarah said to Clara, "Well, it's not like they went and robbed a bank or held up the stage. They were just trying to do some right where a lot of wrong had happened. I for one, haven't seen anything in Festus or Willy, for that matter, that has led me to think they are anything but goodhearted men and hard workers, with the best of intentions in whatever they do."

"Well, that's mighty generous of you ladies," Willy said.

"Sit down," Clara scolded him and Festus. "You men sure do jump to conclusions about us women."

Festus and Willy sat down.

Clara looked at her sister. "Mind, they did just speak the truth." Then she looked at Willy but still speaking to Clara, continued, "It seems to me that what they did was a good thing and it's only right that they got some compensation for doing it."

Looking over at Festus, Sarah asked, "Just how much gold are you talking about?"

He smiled, slightly embarrassed, and looked down at first, then looked her straight in the eyes and said, "There's not enough gold in the world worth losing you over, so however much is there, it doesn't matter if you don't think we should keep it."

"No really, how much gold are you talking about?" Asked Clara.

Willy said, "Like he said, there's not enough gold that would make it worth it to us, if we had to give up being able to stay here with you."

"Okay, we heard that, now tell us, how much gold are you talking about?" Clara said.

Festus and Willy looked at each other and Willy said, "We really don't know the total amount of what it's worth, but we both have three strong boxes of gold coins each," Willy said.

The two women looked at each other and Sarah had to ask, "Just how big is a strongbox, and how much gold does it hold?"

Willy answered, "There's fifteen bags in each box."

"Well, my goodness," said Sarah.

"What we'd like to know is what you think we should do with it?" said Willy. "Since it was originally stolen from the Southern people, we gave back most of it to help those who had lost everything, and just kept this small amount for ourselves, because we also had lost everything. Should we turn it into the Sheriff and let him send it back to the general who really just used the war to steal from people and then the army, or do we try and keep it and use it for ourselves over the next few years?"

Clara and Sarah looked at each other. But they said nothing. Willy could see they were thinking.

"We could bury it out by the stream on your property," Festus said quickly. "Let some time pass and go out and set up a sluice box and act like we're mining in the stream. We could then melt down the coins and claim to have found the gold in the stream, which would give us the right to keep it. We're willing to do whatever you want us to, because we want to spend the rest of our lives with you."

Willy interrupted. "The only way we could feel we weren't living a lie being with you, was to tell you everything, hoping you won't think we are bad people or common thieves. We want you to know ever'thing we've done and hope you can accept us as we are. And we're going to leave it up to you, what happens with us and with the gold."

Finishing he let out a deep sigh.

Festus said, "There it is, we've told you everything and hope you'll still have us."

"Can we see it?" Clara asked. "I've never seen a fifty-dollar gold piece."

"Does that mean…?"

"Of course, we still love you boys," said Sarah.

The two women laughed. "I wish you could have seen the looks on your faces when we got quiet, and you were sure we'd run you outta here," said Clara.

"I want to see it, the coins" said Sarah.

"I suppose you can, but we can't let anyone know that we have it, including your ranch hands. So, we'll have to be careful showing it to you. Come with us over to the wagons and we'll open one of the boxes and show you what's in one of the bags. But you have to act like you're looking at some of the other things that we brought, in case somebody from the bunkhouse just happens to take a look at us over by the wagons."

Willy stood up. He said, "Well, let's get it over with, follow us."

They went out to the wagons, and Willy pulled back the tarp on one. Festus climbed in and opened one of the boxes. Reaching into the box he pulled out a leather drawstring bag and, turning his back so that if anyone was looking from the bunkhouse they couldn't see what he was showing them, he pulled open the drawstring, reached in and pulled out a handful of the coins.

Upon seeing the coins, both women put their hands to their mouths gasping in shock. Clara reached out and took one of the coins to look at, showing it to her sister. Both of their eyes got wide and bright. Neither one could hardly hold back the excitement they were feeling looking at this coin and thinking of the bags that were full of them. She handed it back to Festus and he put it back in the bag. Keeping everything hidden from the bunkhouse, he put it back in the box, then climbed out of the wagon and pulled the tarp back over. They all walked back towards the main house with Sarah and Clara talking to each other in whispers.

When they reached the porch, Sarah collected their cider cups and said, "Let's go inside, I'm not sure I can believe what I just saw."

They all went inside and closed the door. Once inside, the women couldn't hold themselves back.

"Do you realize what that means? Clara said.

"Yes," Sarah said quietly.

They all sat down at the table.

"I thought you said you kept a *small* portion for yourselves. What you have there is a huge amount of gold. You say you have to melt it down in order to be able to claim it?"

Festus nodded, saying, "We don't really know how that works, but we were told by one of our kin that we can melt it like we used to do for our musket balls that we used for hunting back home. He said they mixed it with the dirt from the area where they made their mining claim while it was still a liquid and then dumped it in a sluice box to separate it and then took that to the assayer's office."

"We can't start doing something like that anytime soon," Willy said. "It would be too suspicious for another group of McCoys to have found a mother lode of gold. That's why we thought about going to Denver City or Deadwood, where if that happened it wasn't something that people weren't already trying to do. We can't spend even one gold coin because the Pinkertons have put out word all across the state to be notified of anyone spending gold coins and they have been investigating every report where that happened."

"That's why we thought we would just bury it out there by the stream and we could decide just what we were going to do and when to do it," said Festus. "We want to stop worrying about somebody accidentally finding it.

"So, you've been hanging on to all of this gold and haven't spent even one coin, for how long?" Sarah said.

"Almost a year now," answered Willy.

Sarah continued, "That must be awfully frustrating to have all that gold at your fingertips and not be able to use any of it."

"We just try to act like we never had it and go on living as if we don't, because we never had anything like that in our lives anyway. So, it's not that hard to live without it. What's hard is imagining all you can do with it and then living a meager existence as a ranch hand barely able to feed yourself. We found it best just to put it out of our minds as if we don't have it, until we can get somewhere we can act like we found it. Our solution was to head to the gold fields, wait a month or so, and then start finding small amounts before we hit it big. Then it wouldn't be suspicious, it would actually be what everyone else there was trying to do," Willy explained.

"As far as I know no one has ever found any gold around these parts," said Clara. "If someone were to just up and find a large amount it would not only seem strange, but it would create a gold rush and that would just ruin the territory around the ranch and who knows for how far. We don't really need all that gold, but it sure would be nice to just stop having to worry about having enough food for the cattle and ourselves to get through the winter. I know I've dreamed of just traveling all over the world and having a good foreman run the ranch."

Willy had to warn them, "Some of our kin have already tried this winter to get to Deadwood and Denver City with a very bad results. Five of them have been killed."

Clara and Sarah both brought their hands to their mouths. "Oh no," Sarah said. "I'm sorry."

"Three were bushwhacked by their guides, who were frauds, and two others by marauding Indians," Festus said. "It seems it's very risky just trying to get to where we might be able to turn this gold into money we can use. There's so much riffraff along the way, not to mention Indians. I wonder if it's really worth it to try and haul this gold to one of those places. I know I'd rather be working on a ranch for a living than dead on a trail somewhere. It's not like I've ever known anything different. But I dream about what it would be like to be rich."

Listening and thinking about all that was being said, Sarah decided to say what she felt about it. "I think your plan to bury it out by the stream is a good idea for now, at least until winter is over and maybe we can figure out a way to get it to Denver City or Deadwood safely. Who knows, maybe we can make a claim by our stream and just find small amounts continuously, a little bit every month and it won't create suspicion or a gold rush. I think we need to unload your wagons of your clothes and things and take those boxes out by our picnic area and bury them somewhere above the high watermark, just in case we get a lot of runoff from rains and they won't be exposed by the water washing down the stream."

They all were in agreement. At least for the short term.

Willy looked at Festus. They both said at the same time, "Let's bury it tomorrow."

"First thing," Willy added.

"And I will make sure I send all the ranch hands to work in areas far away from where you'll start digging, to be sure no one accidentally sees what you're doing," said Clara.

They unloaded all their things and brought them in the house and put the tarps back over the wagon beds. The next morning after issuing work orders to the ranch hands, the four of them went out to the stream where they'd gone on their picnic. They searched around for a good area that would be well above the highest high watermark visible along the stream bed.

Finding the spot they all agreed on, the men started digging while the women kept watch. They had brought along a couple of planks of wood so they could slide the boxes down from the wagons, because just lifting them up and putting them on the ground was a difficult job for just two men. Festus and Willy ended up dragging the boxes with their horses and ropes tied to their saddle pommels and the box handles. They buried the boxes about a foot and half underground and marked the top area with some rocks, but not so obvious that it looked like someone was marking the spot. They all rode back to the ranch feeling safer and content that they had done the thing that they all agreed on.

Later, when they were alone, Willy and Festus gave each other a smile.

"I guess it was the right thing to do," said Festus.

"Telling the truth...it's probably always the right thing to do."

Festus nodded. Both men shook their heads, as if they couldn't believe their good fortune, and by that, they didn't only mean about the gold.

CHAPTER 21

A DINNER WITH DETECTIVES

Agent Tucker's other deputies arrived two days after his visit to the ranch. Sunday rolled around and they all made their trip to the McCoy ranch. They rode onto the ranch nice and easy, and dismounted. The deputies waited by the front steps while agent Tucker went up and knocked on the door. When the door opened, he smiled and said, "Something sure smells good," wanting to seem friendly and put the McCoys at ease, all the while hoping that one of them might slip up and say something to incriminate themselves.

James and Junior put extra effort into making this Sunday dinner, because they knew who their guests were going to be. They wanted to make them feel comfortable and not think they were worried about anything; even if the real reason they were there was to try and find evidence against them.

The dinner went well, and everyone had extra helpings of the beef stew and potatoes that they had prepared. Afterwards, some of them were sitting around the fireplace and a few of them were sitting on the porch outside, as it was a nice evening after a rare warm day. Agent Tucker went around to each man and pulled him off to the side to talk to him. After he had talked to all of them and they had all said pretty much the same thing, he thought they had either spent a long time going over what to say should this day come, or they were telling the truth.

He was thinking he should have never put stock in what a thief like Slim said, no matter how bad he wanted to catch those gold thieves.

He sat back down close to William, since he felt he knew William a little better than the others and leaned over towards him, "Well, I have to ask, if you boys had nothing to do with any of this, what are your thoughts on what's happened to the gold and why does it always seem that whenever we find the gold, there's a McCoy or two around?"

William thought about it a moment. Then he got a serious look on his face and looked straight in the eyes of agent Tucker and said, "If it was me that was looking into this, I would go back to the beginning and find out exactly where this gold disappeared from, meaning if the general hired you to find it, there should be a record of it being recovered as spoils of war to help finance the war, and from there I would find out who was supposed to be guarding it or transporting it and turning it over to the Northern Army. That would be a good place to find out who could have taken it. It would have to be someone who knew where it was."

Tucker listened carefully to what William was saying.

William continued, "If it had been taken during transport, then they would have to have known when it was going to be transported, so they could take it in route. You may be able to find out if any of their own soldiers came up with a plan that included outside help to steal it. But the first thing I would do is find out where this gold came from and where it was supposed to have been when it was taken and start from there."

"The thought did occur to me, William," said Tucker. "But you still ain't explained why the gold shows up and your name shows up with it."

William appeared thoughtful. Then he leaned back and said, "As far as us McCoys being around where some of it turned up, it seems that that gold came from a lot of different places that covered a lot of territory and we happened to be living in part of that area and have family in some of the other areas where you ran into some men that had it. It's not our fault that the one's that had it were where we lived or traveled to. Those coins have covered a lot of territory, it seems. I'm not a believer, myself, in coincidence, not too much. If you think about it, it could be almost anyone from those areas. We just happen to be on the move, looking for a better life. And far as I know, that ain't no crime, Agent Tucker."

Agent Tucker thought about this a moment and it came to him that he had never asked his boss if there was a record of this gold ever being reported as recovered from raids and then turned in to finance the war. All he ever did was talk with the general about the areas where it was stolen from, so they could go there and try to find a trail, and where to send it when and if they found any.

The general was the one who was paying his boss to look for it, and they were sending it all to him when they found it. He was pretty sure that his boss would've never questioned the general about the origin of the gold. Surely his boss was assuming the general had authority from the Army to do the investigation, since their own soldiers had turned up nothing. He didn't know if the army was paying the company invoices and the percentage of gold they recovered through the general or if it was being paid directly by the general. He decided he was going to send a wire back to the home office and ask them to look into it with the Department of the Army's spoils of war financing records. Having this thought in his head, agent Tucker decided maybe William was right and the robbery could have been done by their own people.

Either way, it would certainly help to find out exactly how this gold came up missing, who and where it was taken from, and where it came from to begin with. Feeling he had accomplished what he came there to do, he stood from his chair and told his deputies it was time to leave.

He looked around the room and rubbed his belly. "Thanks for the dinner. The food was more than good. And we are much obliged for your invitation."

After they shook hands and said their goodbyes, the agents left and went back to the hotel where they were staying. The McCoys breathed a communal sigh of relief as they watched them head back to town. Sitting around the fireplace they all complemented William for coming up with the idea and explaining it to agent Tucker in such a way that would get the general investigated, knowing he was the real culprit all along, in conjunction with his leaders of the army's raiding groups.

The next day as soon as the telegraph office was open, agent Tucker sent a wire to their home office asking for the information he thought was very important for the investigation at this point. He told them to contact him in Clinton where he had told his other agents to wait for him. Agent Tucker and his deputies left Kansas City and made haste for Clinton, Missouri just after he sent the wire.

CHAPTER 22

FIVE MEN RIDE INTO TOWN

After spending a week at the Braxton Ranch, Festus and Willy decided to go back and visit their kin at the ranch. They were informed about the Pinkertons showing up and what William had told him. They had also learned something else when William went to town for supplies a few days after the Sunday dinner. He found out from the sheriff that the Pinkertons left town, and went to Clinton, Missouri. Relieved that the Pinkertons were gone to Clinton and might be turning the investigation towards the general, they went back to the Braxton ranch with the news and informed the ladies about the latest turn of events. They were relieved because they knew now that they could have been caught red-handed with the gold, had the Pinkertons shown up the day they moved it. It was just sheer luck that they hadn't been there and had gotten away to the Braxton ranch with their gold.

· · ·

It took several days for the Pinkertons to reach Clinton and all along the way, all agent Tucker could think about was what the home office would be able to tell him. He met up with the other deputies and they all got rooms in the same hotel. He went over to the telegraph office and sent another wire asking the home office if they had found out any information about what he had asked. He sent a wire to the general also, asking if he could give him more details about the gold, telling him he needed this information so he could do a better investigation than what they were doing; which was just chasing reports of gold being spent. He needed to find out just where it was stolen from and find the men responsible for guarding it when it was stolen.

After waiting two days, a wire came back from the general stating that some reports of gold coins being spent had come in and it seemed that the men doing the spending were headed towards Clinton. Tucker was disappointed that the general had neglected to give him information about where the gold was originally stolen from and who had been guarding it at the time.

Agent Tucker went to the sheriff and asked him to notify all the merchants, saloons and the boarding houses to keep an eye out for anyone spending gold coins and to get any information to him immediately if someone spent any in town.

"They probably won't stick around very long, and we need to get them while they're here," Tucker told the sheriff.

A few days later agent Tucker got a wire back from the home office telling him that they had inquired with the Department of the Army about the details related to the theft of the gold and were waiting to hear back.

Four days passed with no word and Tucker was growing impatient. Then, on the fifth day, five men rode into town.

These were the five men that had eluded the Pinkertons around Hillsdale Lake a few months before. The men had money to spend so they were not spending any coins, probably change from the gold coins they had spent before they arrived. They were trying to be careful about leaving a trail of gold coins, but their money was running short.

The day after the five men rode into town, Agent Tucker growing ever more anxious to hear from the general or Mr. Pinkerton, received a wire from the home office saying that the Department of the Army was trying to account for the spoils of war that had been turned over for auction and it was going to take some time before they could go through the documentation that they had. The wire continued: "We do not have all the records of the items that were recovered, but the Dept. of the Army should have records of things that were turned in to be auctioned as well as all items that were recovered and were supposed to have been reported and turned over."

Tucker re-read the wire at the end: "I beg of you and your men to be patient while we do the accounting necessary to give you a full and complete answer."

So, Tucker decided to stay put and wait there in Clinton until they either heard of more coins being spent or he got some answers from the home office. He was very frustrated about not getting the information he wanted in a timely fashion, so he went back to the hotel to wait some more.

Then the next afternoon, unknown to Tucker, the owner of a brothel in town paid a visit to the sheriff.

"One of my girls has been paid in a gold coin," she said. "When the man gave her the coin, he made her promise not to spend it until they left town. She assured him she would wait until they were gone. But I had already warned all my girls to keep a lookout for gold coins and not to say anything to anyone if they got one, but to let me know as soon as she did."

The sheriff nodded.

"Right after the man left her room she came downstairs and told me and now I am here to tell you."

"Thank you," the sheriff said. The sheriff got moving quickly and barely got his hat on, before he got on his horse and rode over to the hotel where Tucker was staying.

That day, Tucker was sitting on the porch when the Sheriff brought in the news about the coin being given to one of the women at the brothel. Tucker quickly found two of his deputies and sent them to round up the others and bring them back to the hotel.

Once all nine of the Pinkertons had regrouped at the hotel, they headed together over to the brothel. On the way, agent Tucker decided to position four men—Will, Cody, Jared and Art, in the back and Thaddeus, Dale and Jim across the street from the entrance, while he and Jake would go inside. When Tucker and Jake went inside, the owner quickly found the woman who had reported receiving the coin. While agent Tucker questioned the woman, the other deputy kept his eyes on the other patrons. They noticed that there were two men at a card table playing cards with the resident poker dealer and three others sitting in the waiting area.

As for Tucker interviewing the woman who'd received the coin, she told them that the man had left before she got downstairs and had no idea which way he went or where he had gone.

"For all I know, he could have left town," she said.

The owner told them she never saw the man leave, but between the two of them they gave a fair description of him. Armed with their description they went back outside and regrouped with the rest of the deputies, giving them the information they'd learned.

"Start looking around town and see if you find him and find out if he was with anyone else," Agent Tucker said. "But don't make yourselves obvious."

The men split up into groups of two, and they started going door to door, to every building on both sides of the street. They would go inside the shops as if they were customers, look around and if they found no one fitting the description they would ask the people working there and ask the proprietors if anyone had come in matching the description they had. Not finding the man anywhere, agent Tucker decided they would go back over the town once again.

When they didn't find him, they assumed the man had left town or gone straight to his hotel room. Even though they had checked all the hotels, agent Tucker later reflecting on the events, realized he had actually been in the man's hotel, but the clerk at the desk at the time said he didn't recognize anyone of that description, so Tucker had kept moving down the street.

Back at the brothel, the two men playing cards were part of the group of five that had come into town. They had been very discreet as they listened in on the agent's conversation with the lady. Once the agents had left the place, they waited a few minutes and left themselves, knowing exactly who among them had been the one to give away the gold coin.

They went to the saloon where they knew two of their group would be. Meeting up with them, they told them what they had witnessed in the brothel. Between the four of them they decided that the man who had gained the interest of the Pinkertons was on his own now, and the four of them were getting out of town immediately. They agreed not to let their fifth man know their plans and to try to get out as quietly as possible before they were identified as being with him. They went to their rooms and gathered their things while their associate was sleeping. At the livery they gathered their horses and headed out of town as quietly and carefully as possible so they wouldn't attract any attention. Once out of sight of the town, they started out at a fast pace thinking they would head to Kansas City where they hoped they wouldn't stand out as much in such a big city.

Agent Tucker decided to post Art across the street from the brothel and wait and see if the man came back. He couldn't believe that the man had disappeared, and no one knew where he was. He hoped he hadn't left town already. Once again, they settled in to wait and see. Later that evening the man came down from his room for a bite to eat. The desk clerk saw him and realized he was the one agent Tucker had asked about. He watched him go out the door and quickly grabbed a broom lying beside the entrance door and went outside and pretended to sweep up the boardwalk as he kept an eye on the man. Seeing him go inside the café just down the street, he leaned his broom up against the wall and headed to the sheriff's office.

"I seen the man you're looking for. He's been staying at our hotel. He just left and last I saw he was in the café down the street from the hotel."

The Sheriff thanked the man who hightailed it back to the hotel. The sheriff got on his horse and went straight to agent Tucker's hotel with the news of the whereabouts of the man he was looking for. The other deputies were having their supper in the hotel restaurant, so Tucker was quickly able to gather his men.

Darkness fell and they knew they had to be careful not to let the man slip away in the shadows. Tucker sent one man to retrieve Art, who he had posted in front of the brothel. They gathered across the street from the café and made their plan.

"We want to catch this man alive," Tucker said.

The men nodded in agreement and understanding.

"I want Cody, Will and Jared to go inside the café and find a place to sit as close to the man as possible. Order something to eat."

The three men nodded and hurried over to the café.

"I want Thaddeus and Dale to stay out in front of the café. And Jim and Jake, I want you to go round the back. Stay by the doors. Don't let him get away."

They nodded.

Art, you come with me," Tucker said. "We'll go inside and see how close we can get to him without him getting nervous."

The men all understood. "The idea," Tucker said, "is to surround him but not alarm him of our intentions."

Everything seemed to be going as planned until Will took off his long coat before sitting down at the small table with Cody and Jared. His badge on the lapel of the coat slipped into view for just a second and at that exact second the man they were after saw it glinting in the light.

The man looked around him. Seeing only those three he tried to stay calm telling himself, that of course lawmen had to eat, too. But when agent Tucker came in with his other deputy, the man got scared. Just then the waitress came by his table asking if he needed anything. He stood up quickly and pulled his pistol out, grabbing her and pointing it at her. Keeping her between himself and the five lawmen, he told them, "Keep your hands away from your guns and she won't get hurt. Step aside and let us get by."

The Pinkertons did as they were told, and the fugitive moved around them towards the entrance to the café with his back to the door and the waitress between himself and the lawmen. He went out the door and turned the woman to face the street where the two deputies were waiting.

"Stay where you are and keep your hands away from your guns," he shouted at Dale and Thaddeus.

The two Pinkertons watched, alarmed, as the man kept his gun close to the waitress's head and he dragged her down the steps with him. Looking around, the man took the reins of the nearest horse tied to the hitching post in front and started walking the horse down the street as he walked backwards with the woman in front of him shielding him from the deputies. When he felt he was far enough away that he could mount up safely, he went to the far side of the horse, put one foot in the stirrup holding on to the pommel and slapped the horse. He left the woman standing in the street as the horse started running down the middle of the road. He stayed down below the saddle until he had gained a good distance down the street, then swung himself up onto the saddle bending down low as close as he could get to the horse's neck. Then he took off riding fast, hoping to lose his pursuers in the darkness.

Agent Tucker had been watching from the front door and came running out of the café when the man started off down the street with the horse. He was cursing himself for not going in with guns drawn, but he had been afraid that innocent people would get hurt.

Now they had to hurry to get to their horses and try to catch him before they lost him in the night. The men, all except Dale, ran to their horses, hopped on and took off, but by that time, he was long gone. Dale stayed back to make sure the woman was all right, and to track down the sheriff.

It was too dark to see very far, so all they could do was stay on the road and hope they could hear a running horse when they stopped to listen periodically. No such luck. After a couple of miles, they gave up and headed back to town hoping to try and pick up his trail once it was daylight.

When they arrived at the man's hotel, they checked his hotel room and found his saddlebags with his share of the gold, so they knew they had the right man.

The clerk, a young man, looking dejected said, "Once I recognized that man you were looking for, I went straight to the sheriff and told him."

"It's too late. He got away," Tucker said.

"He was with four other men," the clerk said. "But they checked out and got out of town earlier. Seemed like they were moving quick to me."

Tucker thanked the man, and the man gave them the room keys so they could search where the men had been staying. When Tucker and his men checked those rooms, they found that they'd been completely emptied of everything.

"How do you think the others knew something was wrong?" Tucker asked.

"Maybe," Cody said, "They were in the brothel and overheard us."

Tucker nodded. It wasn't hard to figure out that was probably what happened.

The next day, as soon as there was enough light to see the tracks in the road well enough to follow, the Pinkertons started following the deep imprints of a hard-running horse which gave them a good trail to follow once they were past the main thoroughfare in town. They followed for several miles before the tracks started getting less visible and became normal hoof prints of a walking animal. After about 10 miles they were still following what they thought were the same animal's tracks. It was then that agent Tucker decided it was time to split up.

"Cody," he said, "You and Will and Jared keep following the man."

Cody nodded.

"The rest of you, let's head back to town and see if we can pick up any kind of trail for the others."

When they got back to town they split up and began checking inside shops and restaurants to see if anyone had noticed four riders leaving the day before. Finally, at the end of town, Art and Jake were told by a saloon owner that he saw four riders a little after noon going down the road."

When the Pinkertons regrouped and Tucker learned that four men had been spotted hurrying out of town, he said, "At least we know we have a good possibility of it being the right people, because the time would've been just after the man that got away left the brothel," Tucker told the others.

Agent Tucker went to the telegraph office and sent a wire to the City of Kansas and to Independence, alerting the sheriff to be on the lookout for four strangers coming into town and possibly spending gold coins, telling him they were on their way. They headed out of town in the direction of Independence. After a short distance, they were able to distinguish the tracks left by four horses seemingly traveling together. They continued on until dark and made camp by the road.

The four desperados, once getting what they thought was far enough away from the town, decided it would be better if they split up. Although, they were still going to be headed in the same direction, two of them decided to go to the City of Kansas in Missouri and the other two decided on Kansas City, Kansas. So, two of them stayed on the road, the other two headed out across country because one of them said he knew the way and it would be shorter and safer if they stayed off the road and didn't travel together.

• • •

The three deputies, Cody, Will and Jared, were following the one man who'd escaped the café by holding the waitress at gunpoint.

"He's seems to be heading to Osceola," Will said.

"Sure does," said Cody.

Cody knew that Osceola was the next larger town within forty to fifty miles that did not require crossing the big lakes in the area. The three men rode through Locust Grove after a cold dusting of snow. They stopped to ask around, but no one had any information of the lone fugitive traveling through. As night fell on the second day, they entered Osceola. They decided to get rooms as the temperature had dropped considerably. Going up the steps to the hotel, Cody noticed the horse tied to the hitching post.

"That horse kind of looks like the one I saw him take back in Clinton," he said. "Can't be for sure though since it was dark. But..." he faded out.

The others nodded. Will said, "You might be right. I had a good view of it. It happened fast, but what are the chances, you think?"

The three of them, tired and cold, went inside the hotel.

After putting their things in their rooms, they went back downstairs to the dining room. Walking through the entryway they saw their quarry sitting at a table. He happened to look up at the same moment to see who was coming in and realized who they were. He jumped up and drew his gun. The other diners screamed and ran or ducked for cover. All three of the Pinkertons stopped and drew their weapons.

"Hold it right there," Cody said.

Each man to the right and left took a step towards his side and the man in the middle remained where he was.

"You ain't gonna take me alive," the man said and, at the same time, each of the men fired a shot. Cody was hit in the shoulder by the lone shot the man managed to get off before all three of their bullets hit their mark and the man fell over backwards. No one else was hurt.

"Sorry folks," Will said to the people who had dropped to the floor hiding under their tables. "We're the Pinkertons. You won't be hurt. You can relax now."

Then Jared said to Cody, "You all right?

"Go get the sheriff and the doc," Cody said.

Will kneeled down beside his friend and did his best to stop the bleeding from the wound in Cody's shoulder. He grabbed a couple of cloth napkins and started applying pressure to both sides of his shoulder as blood was coming out from each side where the bullet had passed clean through. It was only a few minutes before the sheriff arrived and shortly after the town doctor showed up. Will went through the man's pockets and found four gold coins as he explained to the sheriff what happened and why they were there, while the doc got the bleeding stopped and said they needed to get Cody into his office so he could clean it properly and bandage him up.

The sheriff asked the manager of the restaurant to get the undertaker and remove the body. Will and Jared helped Cody over to the Doc's place. After getting him patched up they helped him back to the hotel and into his room, bringing him up some hot soup in case he felt up to trying to eat something. There was a telegraph in town and the next morning, while Cody rested, Will sent a wire to agent Tucker, explaining what happened and that they would be waiting for Cody till he was ready to travel. He sent one to Clinton and one to Independence, not knowing for sure where agent Tucker had headed, but figured they were the closest towns, and both had a telegraph.

Agent Tucker and the other deputies: Thaddeus, Dale, Jim, Jake and Art had arrived at the point where the four men they were following had separated, judging from the tracks they found heading off the road. Only two continued forward.

Tucker, who had yet to learn about his deputy, Cody, said, "Thaddeus, Dale, and Jim, I want you to follow these here two tracks that seem to be heading across country."

"Yes sir," they said.

"Thaddeus, I want you to send a wire to Independence or the City of Kansas when you know something."

"Okay, will do." he said.

With Jake and Art at his side, agent Tucker started moving toward Independence thinking to himself that at least this way they outnumbered them by one man.

• • •

Heading northwest the two bandits that broke off from the road were traveling at a trot and making good time. Whenever they got to a rise in the countryside that would allow them to see a long ways behind them, they took a few minutes to scan the areas that they had just passed through. On their second day, they found a good high hill that allowed them to see back almost five miles. One of them, Gideon, had a telescope he had kept with him since the war and was using it to scan the land as far out as they could see. There were small hills and valleys between the horizon and the point they were looking from. At the crest of one of those he saw three riders. He watched them for a couple of minutes. They were not traveling fast so he figured, if they were the law, they were trying to follow the tracks their horses had left. He couldn't be sure, but he decided to err on the side of safety for himself.

Gideon put his telescope away. "I think they're back there, about four or so miles."

"Let's hurry up, then," his partner, Jed said.

They sped up their pace, trying to put more distance between themselves and the three riders coming up from behind. They were letting the horses run at a leisurely canter.

"Hey, lookey there," Gideon said, looking ahead of them.

Jed slowed down. "Looks like there's trees on both sides of the trail there. Now look in the middle, there's an opening between those two thick groups of trees."

The men looked at the thicket. A cold sun shone through the trees, but it was dark and dense.

"Good for hiding," said Jed."

"We need to stop these boys from following us. Let's set up on both sides of the entrance to these pockets of trees after riding our horses between them and a good distance past the area where they start."

"We hide our horses far enough in the trees they can't be seen."

"Then," said Gideon. "We set up an ambush at the beginning of the trees. When they get here, our first shots go to their horses."

"I guess what you're saying is if we can get the horses, they'll never catch us."

Gideon smiled but it looked like a grimace. "Once the horses are down," he said, "we'll try and get the men, but we can't waste much time in a gun battle. I don't want to risk either of us getting hit. If we can't kill them in the first 10 or 15 seconds let's just hightail it to our horses and get the heck out of Dodge. That at least will leave them on foot."

The two men reached the trees and went through the opening. After about 60 yards they each took their own horse off to one side and hid them far enough inside the trees that they couldn't be seen. They then worked their way towards the place where the trees began near the opening where the trail came through.

Jed and Gideon went to each side, and then hid behind the larger trees, closest to their trail. Knowing the men would be following the hoof prints they had left, they settled in at the ready for the riders to show up. They had been waiting over an hour when they saw off in the distance the three riders moving at a fair pace.

"Looks like they figured out we picked up our pace," whispered Jed.

"Get ready! Here they come, don't forget, hit the horses," Gideon shouted. He would only be heard by Jed as the hooves were growing louder the closer they came.

They pulled their rifle barrels back so as not to stick out past the front edge of the tree, while keeping themselves behind the tree trunks so they wouldn't be seen by the unsuspecting Pinkerton agents.

As they got closer to the trees, Thaddeus told the others to be on the lookout. "See these trees. We don't know if these guys will try to bushwhack us."

They slowed down and were walking their horses through the area trying to scan into the trees to see if someone was hiding there waiting for them. Just as they went inside the tree line shots came from both sides, two of their horses whinnied and went down. A third shot came while Jake was looking toward his companions, and he felt his horse go rigid and start falling over. The men were thrown to the ground. Dale and Jim both rolled on impact and came up kneeling trying to see where the shots were coming from. Thaddeus got his leg pinned underneath his horse and was struggling to get out from under it. The next two shots that rang out hit the two kneeling Pinkertons square in their chests knocking them backwards where they landed flat on their backs. Thaddeus saw where the smoke was coming out from behind a tree after hearing the last shots. He pulled his pistol with his leg still under the horse and fired. Bark flew from the tree where the smoke had been. He knew he had missed that one and turned to see if he could see the other one. He only saw a shadow fleeing off in the trees and couldn't get off another shot.

He finally managed to pull his leg out from under the horse and he limped over to Dale and Jim. He checked Jim first and could see the deathly stare in his eyes. He hobbled quickly over to Dale, whose eyes were closed, and checked to see if he was still alive. He shook him a little, saying "Dale, Dale are you okay?"

He noticed the ever growing, dark red stain forming

on his shirt. Realizing both his partners were dead, he quickly dropped down again behind one of the fallen horses and checked the surroundings. Not hearing or seeing anything for a couple of minutes he decided the bushwhackers had bolted out of there. He took stock of the grisly scene.

There were three dead horses and two dead men. He picked up all three canteens, Dale's Henry repeater rifle, as many bullets as he could stuff in his pockets and the one set of saddle bags he was going to take with him. At first, he was going to leave the men there and send someone back to pick up their bodies once he made it to the next town. Then he thought better of it. Knowing that scavengers would tear up their bodies, he decided he would find a way to dig a shallow grave that would hopefully protect them until he could get help to pick them up. He hoped that leaving the horses out in the open would give the scavengers something else to occupy their hunger with.

After he finished with the shallow graves, he looked around trying to get his bearings straight, so when he came back, he would know where to go. After deciding on the landmarks that he would remember, he started down the opening between the trees following the hoof prints of those two bushwhacking varmints. They seemed to still be headed in the direction of Harrisonville, which he figured was about 15 miles away. He was glad his leg was only bruised and that he could walk on it.

Agent Tucker, Jake and Art were almost halfway to

the City of Kansas in Missouri when Thaddeus, Dale and Jim were ambushed. Tucker had no idea that he was down to six healthy agents and one wounded out of the 10 he had originally started with the year before.

CHAPTER 23

LIFE ON THE RANCH

Back in Kansas City, Kansas, Festus and Willy were enjoying life on the Braxton sisters' ranch. They were planning to expand the ranch and take on more livestock. They had talked about bringing in a couple of prized breeding bulls. After many considerations they decided to bring some white-faced Hereford bulls from back east. They had ordered them through a stockbroker and were due to receive them by rail in the next couple of days.

When the day arrived, Willy and Festus left the ranch to fetch the two bulls at the railhead. Everything went fine on the trip to and from the City of Kansas and they brought back two fine-looking specimens to help strengthen their herd. While there in the City of Kansas, they ordered another hundred head of cattle from Texas which would come in the spring.

About two weeks after introducing these bulls to their heifers on the ranch, Willy thought he noticed that some of the cattle seemed to be ailing, right about the time agent Tucker arrived in Independence,

Missouri. Another week went by and they noticed the ailing cattle were losing weight noticeably. By the next week they had three dead cows.

They'd heard the stories of Texas fever among the cattle being shipped back east. That was why they chose to get their bulls from back east so as not to risk the Texas fever epidemic that was starting to take hold in the cattle industry. What they didn't know or realize, was that the disease could be transmitted at the railhead from the Texas cattle being shipped east. They continued to keep checking daily on their herd as they watched one by one the cattle they had, falling sick. They had thought since the bulls weren't ailing or showing any signs of Texas fever that they were okay, and they kept them on the other end of the ranch from the cows. At the beginning of the fourth week, the two new bulls started showing signs of weight loss. The men had a cattle inspector come out and check their herd. He quickly quarantined the ranch and ordered all of the cattle put to death and burned. He had been told by the cattle association that any cattle showing signs of Texas fever had to be segregated and destroyed. The ranches would then be quarantined for an indeterminate amount of time and would not be allowed to receive any cattle until the ranch was given a clean bill of health.

"Oh no," said Clara.

She and Willy were staring out at the horizon after the inspector left.

"We're going to lose the whole herd," Willy said.

"We used practically all of our money to get those

bulls and to order the extra hundred head of cattle from Texas," Clara said. She was the one who handled the accounting for the ranch.

Just then Festus and Sarah walked up. Festus took his hat off and wiped his forehead.

"Word is probably going around about blocking Texas cattle from coming in the territory," Sarah said.

"And we've already paid for the cattle to be brought up," said Festus.

The four of them sat down on the porch and looked out toward the ranch. They were all devastated.

"We might need to get into our gold," said Willy quietly."

They all looked at him.

"It'll be too suspicious," said Clara, always the practical one. "We have to come up with something else."

"No, no," Willy said. "Festus and I been thinking about how to do it. We got a plan that will divert the attention away from us."

The ladies looked at them.

"We'll tell you later," said Willy. He looked at Festus. "Let's go to town."

Willy and Festus went into town and started laying down the cover story with Seth, the general store owner, who they bought their supplies from.

"Hey, Seth," Willy said.

"How you boys doin'?" Seth asked. "Heard you were having some problems with the cattle out at the ranch.

Willy nodded his head. "Guess everyone knows by now."

Seth nodded his head in a grim way.

"We need some supplies," Festus said.

"Okay, how can I help?" said Seth.

They all seemed happy to move on from talk about the cows. Willy told Seth what they thought they were going to need for the sluice box they would have to build for the gold mining operation they were planning along the creek on the Braxton ranch. Seth raised his eyebrows and shook his head, but he sold the supplies to the men.

"Good luck," Seth said. "You'll be needin' it."

Willy laughed along with Seth. "Thank you. We just got no other idea, and we need to replace our cows and the bulls."

"I guess it's as good as any idea," Seth said. "You have a nice afternoon, now."

Word spread quickly around the ranches about the sick cattle. All the nearby ranches and people dealing with cattle in town were beginning to panic about the new outbreak of the disease that was devastating livestock. The neighbors around the ranch had even put signs up and fenced off their property telling any would-be visitors not to enter the property with any animals, horses included. This was because too little was known about the disease and no one wanted to take any chances with their herds.

People crossed the street when they saw Willy and Festus, or when the Braxton sisters came to town. They feared, irrationally, that they would catch something and transmit it to their livestock.

Now after Festus and Willy purchased their supplies, they went over to the assayer's office to see if they could get any plans or books about building sluice boxes and gold prospecting.

They made sure to ask if any gold had been found along the stream that ran through the property.

"Sure has," said the clerk. "A couple sites have coughed up small amounts of gold along the stream over the years, but nothing substantial enough to create a mine.

Another man listening to the conversation said, "A few folks have done some panning in some areas above and below the Braxton ranch's borders and they found small amounts; a few hundred dollars of gold was the most taken from any one spot."

"That's true," said the first man. "But they pulled up stakes and moved on."

They made sure that the people they spoke to understood that this was a last-ditch effort to try to save the ranch and they had no idea what else to try, so this was what they were going to do.

The Braxton sisters told their ranch hands that they'd be able to pay them for a month or two at best, and of course room and board. The men were worried about what was going to happen with them knowing all about the situation with the cattle. A couple of them went around to the nearby ranches only to be held off from even entering the property because of the fear they might be carrying the disease with them. No one was willing to risk losing their herds to take on a couple of cowpunchers from the Braxton ranch. One night the ranch hands talked together about the situation and they decided they did not want to be just taking money for doing menial work around the ranch that wasn't even enough work for two people. They felt they would be taking advantage of the Braxton's.

The next day the foreman came to the main house and told the ladies they were all going to the cattle yard at the railhead in the City of Kansas, Missouri to look for work. If they didn't find any there, they were going to go further east, maybe on to St. Louis, where they were sure to find some work.

"We thank you kindly," one of the men said to Sarah and Clara. Their hearts were heavy. "You've been generous with us these past few years and we feel bad about leaving but we have families. We need to find work that will continue. You understand."

"Yes, we do understand," Clara said. "Thank you for all your help and service."

When they rode off, Clara and Sarah stood by feeling bleak.

"Well," Sarah said. "Looks like just you n' me and the boys are here to resurrect the ranch."

Sarah told Festus and Willy about the ranch hands moving on.

Festus and Willy decided that it was time for them to build the sluice box out at the stream. They had been holding off for fear of the ranch hands wanting to be helpful and trying to work with them searching for gold.

"So, on the one hand it was good the ranch hands have left," Willy said.

Sarah nodded, but she didn't look too happy about any of it.

Festus and Willy took a wagonload of materials and went out to look over the stream to find a site that would be suitable and logical for anyone that came out to inspect the claim they were going to make. They decided on the flat area near where they had buried their gold because of its size, and it seemed logical that there could be gold deposited along the banks whenever high runoff came through and the stream was at its highest levels. Sarah and Clara came out and helped with the unloading and selecting of the spot.

The ladies came out the first couple days with the picnic basket and sat on the stream banks while the men worked. Willy and Festus worked hard to build the box according to the diagrams from the assayer's office and attempted to use it by carrying buckets of water and dumping it in the box.

They did this for three or four days and actually did find a few flakes of gold, maybe $20 worth, which at that time was not bad for a gold miner. There were many times when miners would go three to four weeks without finding any gold. They decided they would take about fifteen coins and use one of the smelting kilns they had bought under the guise of making their own bullets, to melt the gold. They dug up one of their boxes and took fifteen coins from one of the bags and then covered it back up and threw brush over it to hide the disturbed ground. Their sluice box was actually positioned in the stream bed where it would probably be covered with water when there was a big storm, but at the moment the water level was fine, and the area was dry.

They set up the kiln at the edge of the high watermark of the stream bank and leaned one of their muzzle-loaded rifles against a nearby tree and actually had some lead which they used to make a few bullets, just in case someone came by and wanted to know why the kiln was set up. Then they could actually show them they had made some bullets to go hunting since they no longer had any beef or money to buy bullets. They'd just tell anyone who asked that they would have to use their muzzle-loaders to hunt.

When they melted their gold coins, they found the same thing that Wiley had said when he'd done his own gold melting; there was a film of some liquid on the top which they separated and dumped on the ground. The remaining liquid gold they dumped into a hole they had dug on the stream bank that was mainly sand and small pebbles and mixed it around until it cooled and became hard. Then they scooped it up with a bucket and dumped it in the sluice box, sifting out the dirt and small particles that the gold had not adhered itself to. When they were finished, they had a bag of nuggets and small pieces that they were going to take to the assayer's office to ask them how much it was worth.

But first, they would go straight to the claims office at City Hall and file a claim on the Braxton sister's property for their mine. They cleaned off all evidence of the melted gold from the equipment they had used to melt it and packed up the kiln and everything they had used to melt the gold. To anyone coming up on the site it would look exactly the way they wanted it to; as if they'd been panning and sluicing the soil of the streambed.

When they got home that night, they put the kiln and all the accessories in the barn with their old muzzle-loader rifles and pistols that they had kept for emergencies and for memories of home. When they got inside the ranch house, they showed the ladies what they had.

"That's impressive," said Clara with an approving look in her eyes.

Sarah looked at each of the nuggets. "I don't reckon anyone would question these."

For the first time, the four of them felt some hope and they celebrated by opening some of the preserves in the cellar and a nice bottle of wine that had been aging for a long time.

The next morning, they all went into town to file a gold mine claim on the Braxton ranch. They had no idea that agent Tucker was on his way back to their area following the trail of gold coins and the men that had them.

They knew word was going to get to the sheriff quickly about them finding gold and it might seem a little suspicious to him, but they hoped that because the amount was small, he would believe it. The assayer told them that the gold needed to be cleaned up in order to put a value on it, but he would do it for a 15% fee of whatever ended up being able to be assessed.

"Probably between four and five-hundred by the time I finish cleaning it."

They left the gold with him and headed straight to City Hall and filed their mining claim. Having done the most important things they had to do they went to the café for lunch. Sitting in a far corner they spoke quietly among themselves.

"We ought to go to the Sheriff and tell him what we found instead of him coming to us after hearing about it," Willy said.

They all nodded.

"We won't be able to do this too much," Willy warned them. "Maybe not even again. We got to get on our feet is all."

"This should do it," said Sarah in a doubtful voice.

Festus put his hand over her hand. "It will, don't worry."

They left the café and headed over to the sheriff's office. A week had gone by and people in town had calmed down a little. Though the foursome still got some hostile stares, for the most part, the townsfolk had moved on to other issues. Their cows seemed safe, and the quarantine of the Braxton ranch had comforted them.

"Howdy," the sheriff said. "You all look happy and excited about somethin'."

"We are," said Clara.

"What brings you in to see me?" he asked.

"I'm sure you've heard about our situation at the

ranch and maybe even the fact that we are so desperate we started searching for gold in the stream that runs through it."

The sheriff laughed. "Yeah, I heard about that."

It seemed ridiculous to Sheriff Dodd, but he didn't want to hurt their feelings or disappoint them. He remembered some prospectors coming through years before and leaving after they'd only found a few small particles of gold.

"So did you have any luck?" he asked.

"We found a small amount of gold in that stream and we just came from City Hall where we filed a mining claim."

"Well, that's great" Dodd said. But he immediately thought about how the Pinkertons had been looking at them as suspects of the stolen gold.

Willy spoke up quickly, "I know you might be thinking it's an awful big coincidence that the Pinkertons were looking at our family about stolen gold and here we find gold. That's why we came here to tell you first."

"How much did you find?"

Willy shrugged. "We don't know much about gold mining, but it seemed like a small amount."

Festus jumped in, saying, "It's not as if we hit the mother lode or anything. We just wanted to let you know direct from us, rather than hearing things secondhand because maybe it will get blown out of proportion."

"We don't want people piling up and coming on our

land and tearing up that creek," said Sarah. "You understand. We didn't find that much, so better to keep hysteria out of it."

Sheriff Dodd still had a heavily suspicious look on his face. He sighed and said, "I have to say I'm glad you came in here first, but I will need to come out to the ranch and take a look to make sure for myself, not that I have a reason not to trust you but because in my line of work coincidences are always suspicious and rarely a coincidence. Are you headed back to the ranch now?"

Clara decided it was time for her to speak, "Sheriff Dodd you've known us since we were eggs in the nest, and all our lives after. We are honest folks, and we would never lower ourselves or our family's reputation and take up with outlaws. These McCoys are good honest people. We saw them doing the work panning and sluicing the dirt around the stream on our property and watched them take the gold out of it."

Sheriff Dodd's face softened.

"We need to wait until the assayer has finished cleaning up the gold we brought so we can buy some supplies," Sarah said. "After that we'll head back to the ranch. But you're more than welcome to come with us when we're done here in town and you can even stay out at the bunkhouse overnight. Our ranch hands have moved on and the bunkhouse is empty. We can offer you a good home-cooked meal and a nice picnic out at the stream where the claim is and you can watch them work at finding the gold, will that be good enough?"

Sheriff Dodd smiled, he licked his lips and patted his

belly saying, "That's the best offer I've had in a long time and I've heard of your reputation as far as cooking goes, so I'm not going to pass up the chance to get to sample some of that."

Sarah said, "So, then it's settled. When we're finished here in town we'll come by and all ride out to the ranch together. We'll see you later this afternoon."

Then she moved towards the door where Festus quickly opened it for her. They all said goodbye and headed out the door. The Sheriff was left smiling and thinking about the home-cooked meal they were going to give him. He felt better about his suspicions but being a lawman, he still had them and needed to see for himself.

The four of them stopped by the general store and ordered the things they needed to have ready to take back to the ranch. The storekeeper extended them credit and Clara humbly thanked him.

"Our word is good around here," she said. "Don't you worry, we will get you your money in due time."

"I trust you, Miss Braxton," he said. He had been a long-time friend of the Braxton sisters' parents.

Just before they left town, they went back to the assayer's office. Though he wasn't finished he said he knew what he had and how much would be left and told them he would give them $400 now and they could be on their way. They were surprised at how quickly the transaction happened. Clara accepted the money and returned to the store, paying their debt off.

"That was quick," said the store owner.

"I'm a woman of my word," Clara said.

After that they continued on down the street to Sheriff Dodd's office. The two ladies waited on the wagon while Willy went inside. The Sheriff and Willy came out a couple of minutes later and the Sheriff locked his door. He had gone and got his horse from the livery stable, and it was tied up out front, so he was ready to go when they came back. They all headed down the road towards the ranch. The men were thinking of the good dinner the women would make, and the women were thinking of what they were going to make. There was still plenty of daylight and with their fresh groceries, including a fat chicken to roast, they'd have plenty of time to prepare a nice dinner for the sheriff when they got back to the ranch.

• • •

Agent Tucker, Thaddeus and Dale arrived in Independence, Missouri, the day the McCoys went to the assayer's office in Kansas City, Kansas.

The first thing Agent Tucker did was pay the sheriff a visit.

After they dispensed with niceties, Tucker said, "Have you seen a couple of riders come through here?"

"Not anyone that stood out," he said.

"Let me know if you hear anything about a couple strangers riding through town or anyone spending any gold coins. We'll be in the City of Kansas."

"Will do," the sheriff said.

Leaving the sheriff's office Tucker found the telegraph office to see if any news had come in from the home office of the Pinkertons about the origin of this gold they've been chasing.

"No wires for you, sir," the clerk said.

"Mind if I send another one," Tucker asked.

The clerk nodded and Tucker sent a short message that he hoped would make his point. *How long is it supposed to take to get the answers I need? Please send communication to the City of Kansas, Missouri.*

After that, he began checking with all the shops and saloons to see if anyone had traveled through, but no one had seen anyone and no one had any information about the two riders he was looking for. He knew if he wasted too much time in Independence, they risked losing the two men they were following completely. He figured they thought they could get lost in a larger city, so they hadn't even stopped over. So, they went on and Tucker and his men arrived in the City of Kansas after dark the next day. After they paid for their rooms, Tucker looked at his weary men.

"Tomorrow, we will scour the city until we find what we're looking for."

They both nodded.

"Get some sleep, then," he said, and then he went off to his own bed, asleep before his head hit the pillow.

• • •

It took Thaddeus two days of hard walking to get to Harrisonville. Though exhausted, he went straight to the sheriff and told him what happened. When he finished, he said, "I need some help to recover Dale and Jim's bodies."

"Okay,' the sheriff said.

In no time, he had rounded up three horses, one for Thaddeus and two for the dead men, and also two men that would help him.

After half a day's ride, the three men arrived at the ambush site and took note of what the scavengers had done to the horses. They saw that the scavengers had actually started to dig up the bodies but had decided the horses were much easier food to get.

Thaddeus and the two men hauled the bodies back to Harrisonville and buried them the next day. Then Thaddeus sent a wire to Independence, Kansas City, and the City of Kansas hoping to make contact with agent Tucker. So far no one had noticed two strangers passing through, but that didn't mean they hadn't and could still be in town. No one had been on the lookout for two strangers coming in. He decided he would wait for a reply from Agent Tucker. In the meantime, he would check all over town for any information he could get. But first, he felt like he could sleep now for the first time, since giving his partners a decent a burial.

• • •

It was a lot easier in the City of Kansas for two men to go unnoticed. Tucker decided they needed to speak to as many people as possible and hope they could get a thread of information. This was time-consuming but he knew it was his only hope. His optimism might have been ridiculous, but he did want to believe that while his men tried to put some pieces together, he would hear something from the home office about his inquiry to the Department of the Army's "spoils of war department."

The next day he received the telegraph from Thaddeus about being ambushed. After he read it, he sat down for a minute, contemplating the terrible news. After he collected himself, he sent a telegraph back telling Thaddeus to stay put and not confront the men by himself if he found them. He wrote specific orders to make sure he had them well outnumbered with help from the sheriff, before he moved on them. The day after that, he received a wire from Mr. Pinkerton himself, telling him that he was personally heading to the Department of the Army in search of the information.

He said, "I will not rest until we have definite answers," and that it might take him two weeks or more to get it done but he would make sure himself that they had the answers they needed for the investigation. He stated that he was taking a train to Washington the very next day and that he calculated it was going to take him a week to get to Washington and to his appointment with the Secretary of War, Edwin McMasters Stanton. He had garnered the war secretary's attention by requesting information about a large stash of gold coins that the Army had lost. He was going to start at the top to get to the bottom of the mess.

Reassured there would be answers in the near future, agent Tucker sent word to Osceola where Cody, Will and Jared were waiting for Cody to heal up enough to travel. Telling them they had lost two other men, Jim and Dale. He urged them to make sure Cody was well healed before they tried to join back up with him in the City of Kansas. He would concentrate the search between Kansas City and the City of Kansas.

After two days in the City of Kansas without finding out any information, an anxious Agent Tucker, Jake and Art headed to Kansas City, Kansas.

• • •

Sheriff Dodd spent a wonderful evening dining with the Braxton sisters and the two McCoys, gorging himself on the roasted chicken, potatoes, green beans and fresh baked bread. The ladies topped their meal with a fantastic apple pie they made from canned apples from the trees on their property, and some hot apple cider which they drank while sitting around the fireplace.

The next morning, they prepared the picnic basket and went out to the stream where the sluice box was. Arriving at the spot, the Sheriff asked them to wait where they were as he wanted to go ahead and check out their site. He walked around the area inspecting all of the different sites where they had worked. He saw where they dug up the ground, the buckets they used to transport the dirt to the sluice box and their travel back and forth to the stream for the water they needed to pass through the box to sift out the gold ore.

Coming back to them he said, "Let's see you find some more, hopefully. At least show me how you went about doing it and I'll be satisfied."

Festus and Willy went over to the site and started

mining. The Sheriff watched intently, paying attention to their movements and seeing how the process was actually done. They had worked a couple of hours or so and the girls called them to take a break and have lunch. They all sat around the picnic blanket and had a nice lunch.

When their lunch break was over Festus and Willy went back to work and the Sheriff stayed there talking with the ladies. They had sifted through at least fifteen buckets of dirt by the end of the day and actually had found a few particles of gold. They even found a couple of pieces that had been left over from what they had poured in the hole from the melted coins. They put these in a bandanna and took them over to the Sheriff so he could see what their day's work had given them.

Looking at what they had in the bandanna the Sheriff had to admit they got gold from the dirt. Although it might have only been $20 worth, it was still pretty good wages for a day's work,

Sheriff Dodd looked at them and said, "You know, I was really hoping what you were telling me was true, because I like you boys and I think you are honest people and now I believe you actually did get your gold from this dirt. So, thank you for bringing me out here and showing me this, it does my heart good to know I felt right about you all along, and I was."

"Thank you, sir," said Willy. "We appreciate your confidence in our honest work."

"But you know, being a lawman sometimes we're

just too suspicious for our own good and we have to put our minds at ease. And I can tell you, you've put my mind at ease and I'm sure glad of that."

They all rode back to the ranch house and the next morning after a hearty breakfast the sheriff went back to town, feeling content that he had investigated and seen the truth.

• • •

Coming into the city, the first thing that Tucker, Jake and Art did was stop by Sheriff Dodd's office to let him know they were back in town. They said they were following men they had found in Clinton who had some of the gold coins. Sheriff Dodd told Agent Tucker that he hadn't been in town the last couple of days because he'd been invited out to dinner and a picnic with the Braxton sisters and two of the McCoys.

"I'm sorry I wasn't here to be able to tell you whether I saw anyone come into town that I thought might be suspicious, but that doesn't mean we can't take a look around and see what we can find out. We might as well get to looking around, this place is pretty big, probably going to take us a while," he said.

Sheriff Dodd didn't feel he needed to tell him about the McCoy's finding gold, it would just make him suspicious of them for a second time, and he'd have to go through showing them how they found the gold all over again. Dodd thought that would be a waste of time as far as he was concerned, since he was satisfied with what he'd seen.

•••

Thaddeus spent his time in Harrisonville asking all of the merchants and bartenders if any strangers had come through town. On his second day in town, he went to a store that sold food supplies and the clerk, wiping his hand on his apron said, "Two men stopped in and bought some coffee and bacon."

Thaddeus nodded. "It could have been any two men though, right?"

"I know most everyone who comes in here. They mentioned they were heading to the City of Kansas to see about work as cowpunchers with some outfit. But these two men wore their side arms with their gun belts low."

Thaddeus was instantly alerted.

"That made me think they weren't really cowpunchers," he said. "They might have been cowpunchers trying to look tough."

He told him he hadn't thought much about it at the time. "But now after you asking, I remember them, and I thought they were suspicious."

While Thaddeus listened to the store clerk, the two bushwhacking men rode into the City of Kansas from the Southwest, unnoticed by anyone. So many cowpunchers came in and hung around town for a few days that no one would have been suspicious. They would have looked just like everyone else coming into town looking for work. People were getting used to seeing strangers for a short time and never seeing them again.

The two bushwhackers went over to the railhead where most of the cattle was loaded onto the boxcars and asked around if there were any trail bosses still around that might need a couple of hands. They decided to do this in case somebody wanted to check them out. It would back up their story that they were looking for work as cowpunchers.

Everyone they asked told them no more herds were coming until spring. They thought it might be a good idea to try to hide out in the city until spring and then head on to Denver or California when the mountains would be easier to get through. Their problem was they were running out of money and were going to have to use some of their gold coins to be able to stay that long in the city.

• • •

Sheriff Dodd and the Pinkertons spent the better part of three days canvassing every shop, saloon and bordello in town but came up empty. Agent Tucker decided to take his men and head back to the City of Kansas in Missouri. When they arrived back in the City of Kansas, he checked the telegraph office and once again there was no news from the home office. He thought about his lost men, and about Cody's close call. He was feeling dark about the entire thing and wondered if they had died in vain. Cody, who he'd known for a long time was going to get married in the summer, but if they didn't get to the bottom of this, he wondered what would happen to the wedding plans. He was sure Cody's fiancé was always worried about him. And the others who had died had left kin behind, children, wives, girlfriends and parents. For a moment he sat there and let himself feel bad. Then he shrugged it off and headed back out.

• • •

The men started checking in with all of the possible places these men might have ventured into. Everywhere they went people told them that no one really stood out, mainly because they didn't have any real description of these men to offer any aid in identifying them.

Tucker assigned his men certain places to check on a daily basis just in case somebody came in and spent a gold coin. Another week went by and news of one gold coin being spent reached the ears of one of his men. The bartender who had received the coin told them he had never seen the man before and gave them a vague description from what he could remember. Now they knew, at least one of the men was in town. This put them all on high alert and they spent their time double checking everywhere. These two murderers though, were quite adept at laying low and knew how to not draw attention to themselves.

Another week went by before news of another spent gold coin got back to them. Realizing these two men were trying to stay hidden, Tucker wracked his brain trying to imagine where they could be staying so unnoticed for so long. He finally decided they weren't staying in a hotel. They had to be camping outside of town or staying in some sort of a bunkhouse where the cowpunchers would stay when they came into the town. They started checking around the railhead to find out where the cowpokes would stay when they came into town. As cowpunchers, wages were fairly low, and most of them could probably splurge for a single night at a hotel. If they stayed long—and they probably would because it was winter, they moved to bunkhouses.

Tucker and his men found six different bunkhouses that would rent a man a rack for two dollars a week. Four of them were full up and had been that way for the last month. The other two had a few bunks that were empty and had been taking on new borders every now and then for the last month. Two of them had new borders show up in the last two weeks, but at the time they were there asking; the new borders were not present. They stationed one man at each place to keep an eye on who came and went. They compared the men they came across to the description the bartender had given them. They would take shifts of eight hours each keeping watch. A couple more days went by and no one they saw matched the description and no one mentioned that any more gold coins had been spent.

During this time, agent Tucker finally got a response from Mr. Pinkerton. Allan Pinkerton told him that the Department of the Army had a record of some gold coins being confiscated from the South but none ever being turned over as being recovered in raids along the Kansas and Missouri borders. They also stated that the coins that had been sent from Georgia, Tennessee and Mississippi were those that had been recovered during the raids on the plantations in that area and were supposed to have been sent to Independence, Missouri to be used in paying for the war. These were never accounted for. The Army was trying to determine what happened to them during the transport of those coins and so far, the army could only show that they had been sent but there was no record of arrival. They also had no knowledge of the investigation into recovering gold coins assigned to the Pinkertons by the general. This was an undertaking on the generals' part without any knowledge of the Department of the Army.

Now, Agent Tucker had a lot more to think about. He wasn't sure whether he should continue looking for the men that had the gold coins he had been following or if he should go to the general and find out why he had not informed the Department of the Army that they had recovered gold coins during their raids and had received transported shipments of coins from further south.

He also had a big problem trying to figure out how he would face a general in the United States Army. It would be a delicate and uncomfortable interaction. If the general was guilty of keeping those coins for himself, he had to come up with a way to prove it. If he had the coins, Tucker was sure that the general would claim he didn't want to tell the Army about it because he had lost them and was waiting until he had recovered as much as he could, or because he had planned to say they never arrived and he never knew they were coming so didn't know there was something to report, planning on keeping them for himself.

Tucker realized this was going to take a lot more consideration and planning if he was going to find a way to make the general implicate himself without being able to find a way to wiggle out of it. He didn't know whether he should just think of the general as a criminal who stole the recovered coins, or as someone trying to save his hide and career because he lost all of those gold coins while they were under his command. Knowing the general was going to be much more intelligent about covering his tracks or implicating himself if he was involved, Tucker had to make the general dig himself a hole he couldn't get out of if, in fact, he really was trying to keep the loot for himself.

Tucker had only one thing on his side: it had been close to 11 months since the end of the war and the Department of the Army still had no knowledge about this investigation that was started ten months ago, and the shipments that came from further South were never declared to have arrived.

...

The two bushwhackers had decided to spend a couple of nights at a brothel when they cashed one of their coins at the bar. That's why for the two days the Pinkertons had been watching the bunk houses they didn't see anyone matching the descriptions they had. Agent Tucker thought that the men might have left town, so he pulled his deputies off of the surveillance on the bunkhouses. That same day the two scoundrels came back and rented bunks without being observed. Agent Tucker and his men decided to keep checking around town in the various places someone could get a room and stay the night. Two of his deputies found the brothel they had stayed in, but it was too late. The men were gone. They transmitted this information to agent Tucker as quickly as they could. Agent Tucker felt like he was spinning his wheels and those two murderers seemed to just keep one step ahead of them. Wanting to get to the bottom of this investigation, Tucker thought they should head down to Independence and see what they could find on the general. It was now personal to Tucker, because he felt he might have been played by the general. For the moment though, it was more personal to avenge the killing of his deputies.

"We're going to hunt down these bushwhackers before we go chasing any more coins," he told his deputies. "Then I want to pay a visit to the general who started this whole mess. As far as I'm concerned if he hadn't opened this investigation, our boys would still be alive. Let's go back to the railhead bunkhouses and see if they went back there, but first let's check everywhere else in town and make sure they're not somewhere else, then if they're not in the bunkhouses we'll know they left town."

They started at one end of the city and worked their way through it. By late afternoon they had checked all the places that would rent rooms and anywhere someone could pass time during the day. Having not heard any information about the two men, they headed back towards the railhead bunkhouses. Reaching the bunkhouse that was still renting bunks, Tucker stationed his men: Jake at the front and Art over at the corral where the cowboys that were staying there had been allowed to put their horses while they had a bunk in the place. Agent Tucker then went over to the railhead office and asked the foreman if he had rented any bunks in the last day or two and he confirmed that he had just that morning rented two bunks in the very place that agent Tucker had surrounded. Tucker asked him to come with him to the bunkhouse and identify the two men for him.

The foreman had no problem with that. He grabbed his hat and said, "Follow me I'll introduce you to them."

On the way over, Tucker explained to him who he thought they were and that he should be ready for a dangerous situation. Arriving at the bunkhouse, agent Tucker pulled his pistol and held it in his hand down at his side. The foreman didn't bother to knock. He just walked in. Tucker followed.

Tucker immediately spotted the men. They were seated at a table in the middle of the room playing cards with a couple of other cowpokes. Looking up at who was coming in, they realized that it meant trouble for them. They saw that agent Tucker already had his pistol out in his hand but not pointed at them. This made them unsure who Tucker was coming after. But they also wouldn't be able to pull their guns fast enough, if it was them, without getting killed first.

The foreman told them who agent Tucker was. Tucker took over the conversation as the foreman stepped behind him.

"Where you from? What are you doing in town?" Tucker asked.

One of them spoke up, the other remaining silent. "We're from Kansas City, Kansas."

Tucker knew that was a lie, because that's where he had just come from, so he said, "Well, if that's the case then you won't mind me putting my mind at ease by checking your gear and saddlebags?"

"Our gear is out in the tack shed in the corral and so are our saddlebags."

"Then let's go have a quick look and you can get back to your cards," said Tucker.

As the men started to get out of their chairs, Tucker raised his pistol slightly letting them know not to try anything. He then let them lead the way out the door.

When they were outside, the two men saw one man standing off at a short distance watching them. There was another over by the corral. As they started stepping through the fence, Tucker's deputy, Art, who'd been watching the corral, walked over to them. He also had his pistol in his hand but not pointed at them. The foreman stayed at the corral fence and watched as the men walked towards the tack room. Getting to the tack room and stepping inside, Tucker and Jake went in behind them while Art waited outside. The two suspects went over to their saddles that were lying on the floor with their bedrolls and saddlebags. They kept their backs to the door and to the Pinkertons. But this way the agents wouldn't be able to see what they were doing with their hands in front of them. They knew the jig was up and this was going to be their only chance, so standing in front of their gear they reached over to the backside of their saddles and reached inside their saddle bags.

Tucker realized they were reaching inside, and he reacted quickly.

"Watch out," he yelled to his deputy, "Watch out they're pulling guns!"

As the two men stood up, they turned back towards the Pinkertons and both agents jumped to the side, diving behind other saddles and gear, firing their pistols as they dove. The two desperados managed to fire one shot each but hadn't been able to get their aim on the diving Pinkertons, their bullets going through the walls of the tack room. But one of the shots from the Pinkertons did hit one man in the leg. The other shot went wild. After bouncing on the floor behind the saddles, Tucker and his deputy, Jake, who'd been trained well, knew they should never stay in the same place from where they fired their guns. Instinctively they rolled away from where they'd initially dove and fired again, both of their shots hitting their targets. One man was hit square in the chest, the other man, because he had fallen after being hit in the leg, took his bullet in the forehead. No more gunshots were heard and as the smoke cleared, Art, who had been waiting out front, ran into the tack room.

"Thank god you're okay," he said, helping Tucker and Jake to their feet. Tucker told him to check the saddlebags. Inside he found the gold coins confirming these were the killers of their colleagues. The other two men that Agent Tucker's men had been following must have just picked up what they needed to keep traveling and done just that, seeing that they had arrived in the City of Kansas before the Pinkertons. Agent Tucker now had exacted his revenge on the ambush that killed Dale and Jim. Now he had to decide whether he wanted to continue searching for the other two who had disappeared or take a trip to see the general.

CHAPTER 24

THE GENERAL

Agent Tucker decided to send Jake and Art towards St. Louis to see if they could find any information on the last two men he had been following. He was hoping that within a short distance they'd hear news about two men passing through the towns. If that were so, then Tucker would know they were probably headed to St. Louis.

"If you hear anything, let me know as soon as possible," he said to them.

"Yes, sir," they both said.

"If you hear that they've passed through, wire me right away and then head to Harrisonville as quickly as possible.

Yes, sir," they said.

Tucker still wasn't sure how he'd approach the general or make him implicate himself in keeping the missing gold instead of turning it over to the Department of the Army. So, he decided that while Jake and Art were on the trail of those two men headed to St. Louis, he would go down to Harrisonville and meet up with Thaddeus. He wired Cody, Will and Jared in Osceola telling them to come to Harrisonville as quickly as Cody was able to travel. He told them he would be waiting there with Thaddeus for them. He also asked them to collect the gold they had taken off the man they had caught up with and bring it with them. After giving his deputies their assignments, he put the gold in his saddlebags and headed to Harrisonville to meet up with Thaddeus and wait on his other three deputies.

The doc had given Cody permission to travel two days later, after they received their orders to meet in Harrisonville. They would have to travel slowly, so as not to open up Cody's wound. It wasn't the physical pain that bothered him. He was not the type to complain anyway. He just wanted this case to end in justice and see his family and most importantly his fiancé soon. He managed being on the road well—but with the gunshot wound he felt like he was just a bother to everyone. They expected it would take about a week before they could reach Harrisonville. They told Tucker this in a wire they sent to Harrisonville the day they left.

Agent Tucker, knowing it was going to take them a while, took his time heading down to Harrisonville. On his fifth day of travel, he reached Harrisonville and met up with Thaddeus. He got a room in the same hotel and settled in to wait for the others. He spent time with Thaddeus who was mourning the loss of his two friends and while they waited for the others, they could often be seen talking quietly over dinner or smoking on the veranda.

Three days later Cody, Jared and Will arrived with the gold they had taken from the man who had shot Cody. They all stayed in the same hotel and the next day Agent Tucker called them all together to explain what he had found out about the gold. He told them about his correspondence with the home office and then his attempt to find a record of the gold.

"The only records found showed that the gold was supposed to be transported to various holding areas along the Kansas-Missouri border, but no records of it ever arriving were found," he said to the astonished deputies.

"The general," he continued, "had claimed to the Pinkerton agency that the gold was stolen from his transfer stations and he was trying to recover it and return it to the Army."

The men listened quietly.

"The discrepancy is not that the gold arrived, we know that because it was stolen from him. The problem is the gold arrived without being documented," he said. "It was never logged in as inventory awaiting transport."

The men shook their heads. "What does the Department of the Army say?" asked Cody.

"One thing for sure," Tucker said, "Is that the Department of the Army knew nothing of an investigation involving the Pinkertons to recover the stolen gold."

"I wonder what that means," Cody said.

"Exactly," said Tucker. "At this point I wonder what this general is trying to do. I think he's doing one of two things. He knew the gold was stolen and was hoping to find it and return it to the Army, hoping to do so without ever having to record the theft..."

"...Or he wants to make it seem like it never showed up, right?' Said Cody. "That way he can keep it all for himself."

"Yes, that's it, Cody," Tucker said. Then he added, "What we need to do is take this gold we have back to him. We will have him sign a receipt with witnesses, that he has accepted it from me and that it is recovered stolen goods, from the investigation he initiated with us.

The men refreshed their whiskey glasses and lit their pipes. Tucker sat down in a chair for the first time. He'd been standing near the fireplace to stay warm, but now he felt how tired he was.

"After I have the signed receipt," Tucker said, "it will be up to what the general does with the gold and notification to the Department of the Army that will tell us the truth."

The men understanding what he meant, all nodded. He told them they would go to Lawrence, Kansas to the General's ranch, and make the delivery."

"Whatever happens when we get there and after he receives it, is what will tell us what we need to do. I'm going to send a wire to the general and tell him that we are in the area and we're going to drop the gold off ourselves at his ranch."

He looked at his men. Then he said, "Be ready to travel when Jake and Art get here."

The men downed what was left in their glasses, and left the room, clear on their next assignment. When the room was empty and quiet, Tucker looked at his face in the mirror. He felt personally responsible for each and every death that had decreased their numbers as well as for the injury Cody suffered. He sighed, rubbed his chin and suited up against the cold. Beneath the starry winter sky, he went to the telegraph office to wire his note to the general.

CHAPTER 25

QUESTIONS ABOUT A GENERAL

Jake and Art followed the road to St. Louis. When they arrived at Oak Grove, they received notice that a couple of strangers had come through, but the two had spent paper money on their journey. They were almost to the town of Boonville when agent Tucker made it to Harrisonville. In Boonville they found out someone had spent a gold coin for supplies in the general store and bought a wagon from a nearby livery. He was told they left town and headed East with a wagon. They figured the men had bought the wagon to change their tracks and their cover story—where they were heading and why—to throw off anyone that might be following them. Art and Jake thought it would be a good idea to send a wire to agent Tucker explaining the situation and inquiring about their orders. They received a wire back the next day telling them to go as far as Columbia and see if they could catch up with the men in the wagon. Since they were on horseback, they would probably make much better time traveling. They were to notify him of what they found in Columbia as soon as they could.

...

While waiting to hear from Jake and Art, agent Tucker sent a wire to the Pinkerton home office asking if any new information had come in about the general and the gold recovery case they were on. He received back a long communication:

General Ewing was responsible for issuing Gen. Order Number 11; requiring all persons living in Bates, Cass, Jackson, and upper Vernon counties in Missouri to leave the area evacuating their homes and ranches. The order was issued in September 1863.

They were also told that when this took place, 20,000 Missourians were forced to leave the area. The action was meant to stop the guerrilla raids from crossing the borders of Kansas and Missouri where the guerrillas were being helped by the people living in those areas. At the time it was thought to be helpful in combating the raids that were going on against the North.

But the reality was a different story. The raids were retaliation raids for what the North had been doing to the South. It wasn't the South initiating the devastation wrought on the towns in the area.

When the men heard this, they were ever more suspicious of the general. It seemed the order was designed to allow him to continue plundering the valuables so that he could steal them. If there were no people to give resistance, he could easily go wherever he pleased and get whatever he wanted. The order was made under the guise of eliminating the help the guerillas received from the local people; the army would be collecting anything of value that could be sold in auction to help finance the war.

Mr. Pinkerton advised the Department of the Army about the case he had been engaged in by the general to recover gold taken from the Army. Mr. Pinkerton had been told they would do their own investigation as to what was going on. He was told that when the new commander had taken over in Independence there had been no notification of an ongoing investigation or recovery of items stolen from the way stations along the Missouri-Kansas border. As far as the new commander had been informed, everything had been accounted for and the ledgers had been closed out.

Agent Tucker thought deeply about how he was going to get any proof that the general was keeping this for himself and not trying to collect it and turn it back over to the Army. Going over the scenarios in his mind he thought that even though the general had not reported it as of yet, he could still possibly claim he was trying to recover it before he acknowledged it had been stolen so he could save face with the army. As it was, he could say he had never been informed the gold was coming his way, so when it was never entered as being received, he had no idea it was missing until his men had reported the raids to him. He could say he was just following up on the rumors of strong boxes that went missing, hoping to recover whatever he could if it were true. In the end if he was going to try and keep it, it would show up as a discrepancy in the transportation manifests of shipments coming from further South destined to be auctioned in Independence or sent on to the Department of the Army's spoils of war fund that never had arrived to him, which had been known to happen and that would be long after he was gone from the military.

The general could claim he had heard stories of the shipments and was just trying to see if there was any truth to the rumors by doing this investigation. There were no records or receipts with his signature on them anywhere, and the only signatures that would be found would be those of the two men who had been doing his bidding; they were the only people that had ever sent or received telegrams, or signed for anything that had been recovered, thus making it possible for him to deny any knowledge of it.

It seemed to Tucker that a man of the general's stature who had advocated for Kansas to reach statehood and wanted to be part of the political framework of the new state was not a man out only for his own benefit. It just didn't fit together. The only thing that agent Tucker could come up with, that made any sense was that possibly the general was completely consumed with wanting power and wealth and thought the gold was his way to assure having it. The one thing he knew was that his agency had receipts for every bit of gold turned over to all of the sheriffs in the different towns where they had recovered it and that someone would have signed for it when those sheriffs turned it back over to whomever was claiming it. Whoever did that, would be held responsible for the gold. Tucker had only received orders from Mr. Pinkerton and communications by wire supposedly from the general. He had never spoken face to face with the general about any of it.

Tucker sent a wire to a couple of towns where they had left gold that they recovered when they first started on the case. He sent the wires to the sheriffs asking them to confirm the amount of gold that had been picked up and returned to the general. He also sent a wire back to the home office of the Pinkertons explaining his idea of drawing up a receipt for the general to sign, documenting that he had engaged them in recovering the gold, and noting the amount he was turning over personally. He also documented what had been turned over to the different sheriffs across the state of Missouri and what the corresponding receipt amounts were for the money the sheriffs had turned over to the general. He thought if he could get the general to sign the paper himself, in front of him and his deputies, then he would have hard evidence that the general was involved and receiving the gold being recovered. He decided he would find a lawyer to draw up a formal receipt with all of this included in the document. After sending his wire, he went directly to the sheriff to ask which attorney he would recommend to do this. The sheriff told him he knew one lawyer that was really good at drafting contracts and deeds and thought that he would probably be good at drawing up a formal receipt. He also told him that he was very honest and would keep client confidentiality, so word wouldn't get to the general about what was being drawn up for him to sign.

• • •

Two days later, Tucker received a wire from Jake and Art telling him that a couple of strangers had gone through Columbia and seemed to be headed to St. Louis. They asked for his instructions on what they were to do from there. He replied for them to come to Harrisonville because he thought he might need all of his men when going to the general's ranch to bring him the gold they had in their possession. He asked them to make their way quickly to him.

He knew it would take probably a week for Jake and Art to get there. A couple of days later he received the wires about who had picked up the gold and signed for it. When he didn't recognize the names, it confirmed his suspicions. The general was trying to keep his name out of it.

Tucker hoped for a response from the Department of the Army about their investigation into this situation. His desire was that they take the investigation over from him, telling him to deliver the gold to the new general in Independence that he was planning on returning to General Ewing and they would take over from there. Unfortunately, the bureaucracy within the military and the slow communications between the different departments made it certain he would not receive any help or communication from them before his men arrived in Harrisonville.

Chapter 26

Spring

March arrived and by the middle of the month, the weather had started to warm up. The McCoys back in Kansas City, Kansas were starting to get anxious to get some place where they could use their gold. Willy and Festus were enjoying their life on the Braxton's ranch and the four of them had decided that whenever they were in need, they would only meltdown enough gold for what they needed at the time. That way they could continue building the ranch back up while spending as little gold as possible. Since they had no idea when they would be able to get the cattle they had ordered from Texas, they had ordered 50 head of cattle, two breeding Bulls, and 20 horses from a place in Virginia and felt certain this time they would not contract Texas fever. They made one more trip to the assayer's office with gold from the stream in order to pay for them and the feed that would be needed for them when they got there. They made sure they had enough money left over to buy the supplies they needed while they waited for the animals to arrive. One day,

Festus and Willy were sitting on the porch. The sun had warmed up some and for the first time, things seemed to be thawing out.

"So," Willy said. "What do you think. You gonna propose to Sarah?"

Festus looked over at Willy. "I was gonna ask you the same question about Clara."

The men laughed.

"I got no idea if they been thinking about matrimony," said Willy. "What about you?"

"Nothing. Sarah hasn't said a thing, I don't know if she's waitin' on me to ask her.

The men fell silent. Willy looked around him and realized how good life had been. He finally broke the silence.

"I think we both should propose."

Festus sat back in his chair. "All right then. Let's do it."

• • •

Billy and William signed on with Dusty Trails for his next caravan heading to Denver City, which was supposed to leave at the end of the next week. Jonesy, James, and Junior opted to go to Deadwood with Mountain Man Sam. Sam acquired four other customers that wanted to leave at the end of the week, and he invited those McCoys who wanted to be part of his group to come along at half-price. He still felt bad about what happened on the last trip he made with the McCoys. Everyone was getting eager to get to where they could actually start new lives using their gold. The lovely warm spring days only made them itch more to get on with their lives.

The McCoys back on the ranch in Lawrence, Kansas made it through the winter and were waiting on the new livestock that was coming to the ranch from orders they placed with the money Wiley had sent them. They'd each have 500 head of cattle and 50 horses as their share of the ranch without having to use any of their buried gold. They would have their hands full trying to keep up with all the work that would be demanded of them. They looked forward to having the work to do because they knew they were all working for themselves and building a future for all of them. Their dream of a ranch run by their family and profiting equally was about to begin.

• • •

Tucker gathered all the information he'd collected and took it to the lawyer to include it all in the receipt to be drawn up while they waited in Harrisonville. Jake and Art showed up another four days later. Now Tucker had his whole squad with him. He picked up the receipt the lawyer had drawn up for him and totaled up the amount of gold they were delivering personally and put it in the blank space. The receipt also showed a tally of the total amount for the receipts they had received from the different sheriffs who received the recaptured gold and had turned it over to the general's men. Tucker was quite surprised at how large the sum turned out to be. That amount of gold would make most people think twice about how they might be able to try to steal it and keep it for themselves. When he was certain all the paperwork, and his nerves were ready and steady, he told his men they would be leaving in the morning to see the general.

The next morning, cold enough that they could see their breath, the men divided the gold between them and placed it in the saddle bags each deputy carried, and they started out on the road to the general's ranch. They made it to Lawrence just after dark and put their tired horses in a livery nearby and then paid for their hotel rooms. After the long hard ride to get to Lawrence, agent Tucker needed to have his men and their horses fresh for when they went to see the general, not knowing what kind of a situation they would be getting themselves into. He decided they would stay one day in town and ask around about the general's activities and see what they could find out.

After breakfast the next day, Tucker noticed how the town seemed to be booming with construction. The deputies were divided into three groups of two men each and each group went around town gathering information about the general.

Agent Tucker visited the sheriff and from there went to the telegraph office to notify Mr. Pinkerton that tomorrow he would see the general. That evening, when they all gathered for supper, they shared the information they had collected.

As it turned out, the general had been building a ranch the size of which no one had ever seen in the area, and bigger than most in the whole territory of Kansas for that matter. He was hiring as many men as he could find to carry out the work on the ranch. He was no longer with the Army, but still donned his uniform on most days. He was proud that he had served and that, at one point, he had been a commander for the entire area. He believed that while he wore his uniform, he commanded more respect from the men he came into contact with and parried more favor from the women who passed him by. To General Ewing, the uniform also gave him a superior attitude, as if he had earned the right to so much ego and stature and he harnessed that to command all those who were working for him and to give him a sense of power and importance when he went to town on business. People feared him and others called him a narcissist. No one was comfortable with one person having so much power. And the general never believed that he needed to consult with anyone about his decisions. Much of the time his decisions were self-serving, and they hurt the people around him. But he seemed not to care.

Having been directed by the Sheriff on how to find the general's ranch, it only took Tucker and his deputies a couple of hours to reach the gates. Way off in the distance they could see the buildings of the main ranch house and barns. It was truly a grand site. They were glad it was not too cold at midmorning when they tied their horses off to the hitching post in front of the main house; a mansion that was so big it offended many of the humble townspeople who worked hard for low wages.

One of the general's guards that stood sentry on the

wide porch had gone inside to inform the general that he had visitors. The general appeared on the porch in his uniform and noticed the badges on the men in front of him.

"Well, I finally get to meet the men responsible for returning all this gold," the general said. "It's a pleasure to actually see your faces. Can I get you all something to drink? I have fresh coffee and some nice cool well water. What can I bring you?"

Agent Tucker responded, "We don't have much time, General. We're on our way to St. Louis, where the last few men we know about carrying some of this gold, are headed. We hope we can catch up with them there. So far, we haven't heard about any more gold coins being spent anywhere. I thought we would just deliver what we have on us, directly to you, since St. Louis is going to be a pretty far trek. We don't need to be carrying all this gold around."

The general smiled in a way that made Tucker wonder if he was thinking about the gold he was about to receive and add to his fortune. "Why don't you boys come up on the porch and have a seat, while we do an inventory of what you brought. I'll have the cook make up some fresh coffee for us."

Agent Tucker didn't want to pause for refreshments, but he wanted to keep the general at ease, so he said, "All right then, you've convinced me. That's right kindly of you sir, I'm sure the boys are a little bit parched. I know I could use a cup. Come on boys, pull up a seat, while the general and I take care of business."

"Why don't we go into my office Agent Tucker, I would prefer not to conduct our business out here on the porch."

"Sounds good to me," said Tucker. Then to his deputies he said, "Boys why don't you bring those saddlebags into his office for me and then wait out here on the porch till we get finished."

The general showed them the way and agent Tucker watched while the men deposited the saddlebags in front of the general's desk and went back out to the porch.

The general told Tucker to have a seat in the fancy, elegantly tooled leather chair in front of his desk. The room was very beautiful with wainscoting and fresh paint. A large window looked out on the ranch. The general's desk was made of fine wood, stained a dark brown, and like everything else, seemed bigger than was necessary. On the wall were photos that Tucker thought must have been of his family members.

Agent Tucker sat down, making sure to sit on the front half in case he would need to jump out of the chair quickly. The general noticed the serious look on Tucker's face.

"What's on your mind?" the general asked. "I can see something is troubling you."

Tucker gave the general a direct, serious look right into his eyes, as he started to speak. "Well Sir, I just want you to know that my deputies and I have worked very hard on tracking this gold down. Some of them even gave their lives. Although I know that's part of what we have to expect in this business, it's still hard for me when I lose one of my men, let alone three. I have another one that may not be able to use his gun very well ever again, due to taking a bullet in the shoulder. This case has taken a big toll on me and my men, and I'm hoping it's going to be over real soon."

The general thought about what Agent Tucker had just said. "I'm sorry that you lost men over this gold and I would've hoped that no lives were lost while pursuing this case. I can't do anything about that, except tell you that I'm sorry for what's happened and to express my gratitude. I do believe there's still more gold out there, but it's probably long gone and whoever has it is being smart enough to not leave a trail."

Tucker wasn't impressed by the general's answer.

"I have actually left the army," the general said, "and have been very active and determined in petitioning for myself to be the state representative for Kansas and trying to build my ranch while you've been doing this investigation. We've both been very busy doing what we think is right. Let's get this business over with so we can go back to doing just that."

"That sounds fine to me," said Tucker. "You'll need to count what we brought and then you and I need to sign a receipt for receiving it."

He reached inside his saddle bag for the receipt the lawyer had drawn up.

"I'm sure it's all there," the general said, "and what you have on the receipt is going to be accounted for, so I'll just sign the receipt and we can both get about doing our business."

Agent Tucker found the general's behavior suspicious. Why was he in such a hurry? Tucker handed him the receipt. As general Ewing unfolded the paper and spread it out on his desk, he realized this was not just a regular receipt he had in front of him. Reading the papers, he saw that what he was actually signing stated that he had initiated the investigation and had received all of the other gold that had been recovered plus what they had brought today. He noticed it was also in triplicate and that the copies would be sent to the Army, the Pinkerton files, and to him.

Agent Tucker saw the new troubled expression on the general's face after he read the document. He realized he was the only one present to witness the general's signature and asked the general to wait a moment before signing the document.

"I need to have at least two other witnesses to confirm you signing the document."

Without waiting for reply from the general, Tucker went out to the porch and asked Cody, Thaddeus and Jake to come inside for a moment. When all four returned and stood in front of the desk, agent Tucker told the general, "Okay you can sign the receipt whenever you're ready."

• • •

The general was clearly quite nervous, and he knew it was showing on his face. What did it mean that he would be signing this document? He also realized he had no choice. If he didn't, he would be considered a thief and a war criminal and his whole life would be ruined. He was also thinking about all the money he had spent for everything he had been doing the last year, which had come from the gold that had been recovered which he had tried to keep for himself. He was going to have to find a way to cover all that money because now, minus the expenses incurred by the Pinkertons and their fee, all of the gold that was on this receipt would have to be turned over to the Army.

He would have some time to come up with all the money, but it was still going to cost him dearly. His income was nowhere near what he had spent building his ranch and political reputation. He didn't know at the moment what he was going to do, except that he had feared at one time in the future this was going to catch up with him. Now that it had, he had to save his reputation if he had any aspirations of continuing as a politician. He would just do whatever it took to keep himself out of prison and to keep his name and reputation as being an honest man, fighting for the rights of the people and the good of the territory. He was hoping now that he wouldn't go broke before he could be nominated as the state representative of Kansas.

• • •

The four Pinkertons stood by watching. Tucker noticed that the general seemed lost in thought. He saw the general's face change as the reality of his situation began to sink in. When he finally resigned to the fact that this was actually happening, he took a deep breath, straightened out the receipt while holding it firmly on his desk and signed his name. Once his signature was on all pages of the document, forgetting all about the fact that Agent Tucker had to sign it also, he folded it back up and handed it to agent Tucker with a defeated and disappointed look on his face as it exchanged hands. Tucker took it back to his desk reopened it and signed it himself, then gave the general his copy. He then folded the other two copies and putting them in his vest.

The general looking kind of pale said, "Well gentlemen, I believe this concludes our business and I want to thank you for all your hard work and trouble."

He reached out to shake hands with Agent Tucker and the other three deputies. When this was done, the Pinkertons turned and headed back out onto the porch and to the fresh coffee that was waiting there.

It was several minutes before the general joined them on the porch, and when he did, he said, "Might I have a private word with you, Agent Tucker."

The men exchanged quick glances as Agent Tucker followed the general into his office. The first thing he noticed that was different, was a Bible open on the desk. As the general approached his big, expensive desk, he made a point of picking up the Bible, folding it closed and putting back on the stand in the corner of the room. It was then that Agent Tucker began to think that the general had decided to stay an honest man—or maybe it would be more accurate to say, return to his old life as an honest man.

"Please," the general gestured for the chair opposite his desk, as he sat down.

When they were both seated, the general took in a deep breath. Then he said, "I think from this point on, this investigation will be taken on by the Department of the Army, since I am no longer part of the Army."

Agent Tucker nodded his head.

"I'm sure they will be in contact with your home office, if they intend to pursue the investigation," the general said. "But as of now, I am not going to continue pursuing this, and I will notify the army as such, as I have many other things I have to conclude, and I shouldn't have to concern myself with this anymore. I will send a wire to your home office containing my statement."

Agent Tucker nodded his head. "I understand, Sir," he said.

"Good," said the general.

The men stood up. The general put his hand out and Agent Tucker took it.

"I am a man of my word," said the general.

"I appreciate that," said Tucker, relieved that the general had decided to make good on what he had done. Even though, in the beginning, the general had probably thought he would get away with stealing, it was clear that he now realized he had no choice but to turn over the gold to the Army and declare that he had been trying to recover this gold on his own, so that it would never put a blemish on his military career.

Although being late in declaring that he had started the investigation and had been collecting the gold, which would make them suspicious as to his real intentions when he started, he would be turning it over to the Department of the Army now.

"If there are any…accounting issues, of course, I will make all restitution," the general paused to cough, "for what might be missing."

Agent Tucker nodded.

"You may see yourself out," the general said.

Without another word, Tucker left the office, allowing the general the dignity not to have to face him or his men again. As Tucker rejoined his men, he nodded, and they all seemed to understand what had happened. He figured that the Army probably would not charge him because he voluntarily told them about what he had been doing and gave back what he had recovered, giving him the benefit of the doubt because of his military record and as being the first chief justice of Kansas, as well as being a Free State advocate, as long as he paid back what was missing. As they rode off, Agent Tucker looked back and saw the general standing on the porch. He saluted the general as he rode away.

EPILOGUE

In the months that followed, the Army decided to do what agent Tucker thought they would do to the general. They closed the investigation into recovering any more of the gold and made the general pay restitution for what was unaccounted for. In order to do this, the general had to sell everything he had in Kansas, leaving him almost nothing. He did not receive the representative status he had hoped for in Kansas, probably due to the General Order 11 that he had orchestrated during the Civil War, and because of the gossip and suspicions about the stolen gold. He still had large debts to pay back when he moved on to Ohio where he became a United States Congressman. He almost became governor of Ohio in 1880 but lost the election.

The Pinkertons returned to their home office in Chicago, Illinois without heading to St. Louis to chase after Big John or the two men that had bought a wagon and headed in that direction. Tucker and his men believed that if no one else wanted to pursue the missing gold there was no need for them to do it either. Cody would never be able to shoot accurately again because of his wounded shoulder. He married his fiancé and become involved in the local politics of his town.

None of the McCoys would likely ever know that they no longer had to look over their shoulders for the law. Since this information would probably never reach their ears, they had to conduct themselves as if the investigation was still going on.

Willy and Festus married the Braxton sisters and continued their life on the ranch melting down only what gold they needed, in hopes that one day the ranch would be self-sufficient, and they could leave the rest of the gold alone, buried where it was.

Billy and William made it to Denver City under the guidance of Dusty Trails and found a place to stake a claim for a gold mine and were about to find out what that really meant.

Jonesy, James and Junior made it to Deadwood thanks to the help of Mountain Man Sam. They only ran into the band of Indians that Sam had been trading with on a regular basis. This time they all made it through, and they had found an area where gold had been found some time before, but the vein had played out. They moved upstream almost a mile from the area and made a new claim of a gold mine. The area quickly became overrun with miners struck by gold fever.

They now had a lot more to worry about than they had ever imagined. Having all this gold was turning out to be a lot harder than they expected. They now had danger at every turn and couldn't trust anyone but themselves. The two groups of McCoys; Billy and William in Denver city and James, Jonesy and Junior in

Deadwood, hoped they would get all of their gold melted down and turned into the assayer's office before any of them got killed. The plan was to do that and then get the heck out of the area and find a place to live where no one knew them.

Whether or not they were able to reach their goal, and what happened, continues in the next saga of the McCoys before the feud.

ALSO BY THOMAS MCCOY

IN THE *MCCOYS BEFORE THE FEUD* SERIES

Before The Feud (Book 1)

A corrupt general. A stockpile of plundered Southern riches. Can a proud family reclaim the gold for its rightful owners?

Kansas-Mississippi border, 1865. Tommy McCoy burns for justice. Reeling from the end of the bloody Civil War, he learns that a corrupt Northern general has raided the bounty of the Confederacy and plans to keep it. Tommy and his shrewd father vow to get back the valuables for innocent Southern families or die trying.

With time running out before the general's reinforcements arrive, Tommy risks a deadly confrontation in a series of secret raids. Can he secure the rightful Confederate property before the North deals the McCoys a final crushing blow?

The McCoys: Before the Feud is the first book in a deeply-researched historical Western saga. If you like dusty battles, a different point of view on yesteryear, and twists you won't see coming, then you'll love

Thomas A. McCoy's gripping tale of justice for the people.

Buy *The McCoys: Before the Feud* to join a family's quest for justice today!

Home To Kentucky (Book 2)

A treacherous journey. Wagons packed with gold. Will the McCoys outrun a group of lawmen or swing from the gallows?

Kansas, 1865. Wiley McCoy can't wait to return home. He counts down the days until his family can stop laying low and return to Kentucky with the rightfully plundered valuables they took back for the South. But crossing the open prairie with four wagons full of gold may bring Wiley a lethal set of new problems.

With desperate outlaws and opportunistic deserters at every turn, Wiley and the other McCoys must watch their backs to survive. But they never expected their greatest enemy to come in the form of ten brilliant Pinkerton detectives…

Can Wiley make it home before the lawmen slip a rope around his neck?

Home to Kentucky is the second book in The McCoys: Before the Feud saga of historical Western novels. If you like determined heroes, realistic Southern settings, and quests for justice, then you'll love Thomas A. McCoy's treacherous wagon ride.

Buy *Home to Kentucky* to ride along with the McCoys today!

Back at the Ranch (Book 3)

Southern honor. Northern greed. The cost of failure could be their lives...

Kansas, 1865. Tommy McCoy sees a bright future ahead. After succeeding in several risky raids to reclaim the South's gold from a thieving Union general, he's finally back home with the woman he loves. But when Pinkerton detectives start snooping around, he's worried his temporary comfort will end with an execution.

To keep his family safe, Tommy devises an ingenious but dicey plan to protect his family from suspicion. After some of the McCoys refuse to take part in the high-stakes scheme, Tommy may lack the men he needs to outmaneuver the law one final time...

Will Tommy evade the Pinkertons or will his family's rightful property fill a corrupt general's pockets?

Back at the Ranch is the third book in the *McCoys: Before the Feud* historical Western saga. If you like go-for-broke action, clever twists and turns, and good people fighting for what's right, then you'll love Thomas A. McCoy's riveting adventure.

Buy *Back at the Ranch* to witness real McCoy ingenuity today!

ABOUT THE AUTHOR

Thomas Allan McCoy is the author of the Western Historical Fiction series *The McCoy's: Before the Feud.* As a direct descendant of the original McCoy family that was involved in the legendary feud between the Hatfields and McCoys, he provides a unique perspective and valuable insights regarding their traits, morals, and how family honor affected the way they carried out their lives after the Civil War. Inspired by the dramatic events that occurred within his own family history, McCoy weaves together facts and fiction to bring to life events that were happening in our country before this timeless feud from the 1860s took place.

McCoy's father, grandfather, great, and great, great grandfather were all born in Pikeville, Kentucky. However, he grew up in Southern California. In addition to writing, McCoy loves fishing, traveling, and baseball. He now lives in Arizona with his wife.

Made in the USA
Columbia, SC
26 December 2021